SECRET KILL

NOIR NIGHTS BOOK 2

ROBIN STOREY

For Aaron, as always

CHAPTER ONE

The plastic chair dug into my butt as I sat in the back of the conference room. I ran my fingers around my neck inside my shirt collar. The air-conditioning was arctic, but my neck felt as if it were on fire and itched like crazy.

I willed myself to stop scratching. Sometimes my whole body itched with the sensation of insects crawling over me. My doctor had told me it was stress and advised me to take up yoga and meditation. I threw the pamphlet for the Serenity Yoga School at him and stormed out.

I tried to concentrate on the director's speech as he rabbited on about the importance of young people who'd taken the wrong path in life (he avoided the word criminals, all very P.C.) being given the chance to make a fresh start.

I'd heard it all before, several times. Every time New Life Inc. had a new intake of participants, they invited me for morning tea and asked me to give a speech. They called them students, but whether they actually learned anything was debatable.

'We're very honoured to have as our guest, the patron of our organisation, the managing director of Palmer Product Packaging, Mr Jackson Forbes.'

I got up to a thin round of applause and walked up to the front of the room. Richard returned to his seat at the back of the room next to Matthew, the program facilitator. Seated around the table were a dozen young people, from late teens to mid-twenties; ten men and two women. They slumped in their chairs, blank-faced and fidgety. A lank-haired girl picked at the scabs on her arm. The boy beside her, his pale arms like ghostly twigs protruding from his stained T-shirt, regarded me with a twenty-cones-a-day gaze.

A beefy lad directly on my right placed his hands on the table, making sure I saw the words tattooed on his knuckles. Death and Anarchy. I could read all their thoughts as if they were in one giant thought bubble—'What's an old fart in a suit got to say that I'll give a fuck about?'

'Thank you for that warm welcome, Richard. Please call me Jack—Jackson sounds like your local coffee shop guy whose name tag says Awesome Coffee Ninja and wears his hair in a topknot.'

That got a few sniggers. I gave my usual speech about growing up in a public housing estate with a violent alcoholic father and clinically depressed mother, spending my childhood dodging fists and broken bottles and saving my mother from Valium overdoses, finding refuge in crime and drugs with my older brother Sam and the neighbourhood kids. A story, or variations of it, familiar to most of them. Then seeing the light at 24, leaving Sydney for Melbourne and spending three years doing shit jobs before finding something that I could even remotely imagine myself liking.

I didn't go on with the 'rah rah if I can do it, you can do it' kind of stuff that some ex-cons do. I just gave them the facts and let them draw their own conclusions. When I finished, I studied their faces. I knew what they were thinking. 'It's all right for you, you just got lucky. There's no way I could ever get to where you are.'

It's true that I did get lucky when I met Lindsay, whose father was the owner of Palmer Products Packaging, a multi-million dollar business that his father had started in his garage. But that was just the beginning of the long road to the top. Old man Palmer didn't give me any slack—he came down on me like a ton of bricks at every opportunity. And that luck wouldn't have found me if I was still doing drugs and crime.

'Anyone got any questions? I asked. Silence while they squirmed in their seats and looked down at the table.

'What prison were you in?' Tattooed Knuckles finally asked.

'I didn't go to prison. Some of the crimes I committed I didn't get caught for, but I was well and truly on the road to getting there.'

His expression said it all. If you haven't been to prison you're not a real crim.

This paved the way for the others to pepper me with questions. What drugs did you take? What crimes did you do? What happened to your friends? And your brother?

I knew why they were asking those questions. They were trying to bring me down to their level—to find some way of relating who I used to be to who they were now.

When the flurry of questions died down, Richard was half out of his seat to do his thank-you speech, when a young guy put up his hand. He'd been silent up until now listening to the others. There was something still fresh and innocent about his face, and it wasn't just the crop of pimples on his chin. I guessed that he was fairly new to the game, maybe hadn't even done time. But if there was any hope of him getting out of crime, he needed to stop hanging around with these others. That was the problem with these programs, worthy as they might be in theory. Hanging around with other crims was not the best way to get straight.

'Why did you decide to stop doing crime? Did you like wake up one morning and decide you'd had enough?'

I wished I could tell him the real reason; maybe it would make Tattooed Knuckles sit up and wipe that sneer off his face. Instead I nodded. 'Something like that. I was in court on a stealing charge and the magistrate told me if I came back before him again he'd send me to prison. To my mind, that was the worst thing that could happen to me, so that was my wake-up call. But that moment when you to say to yourself, "I don't want to do this any more" will be different for every person. Your determination must be strong because it's not easy. There'll be times when you'll be very tempted to slip back into your old life.'

The kid didn't look completely satisfied with my answer, but before I could elaborate any further, Richard stood up. 'Thank you very much, Jackson, for an inspiring speech. I'm sure you've given everyone here food for thought. And speaking of food, let's have some morning tea.'

We stood around and drank instant coffee from styrofoam cups and munched on cardboard biscuits, the students in one group and Richard, Matthew and I in the other. The young kid didn't look my way once; he was absorbed into the group, nudging the scabby-armed girl and laughing loudly at some joke that Tattooed Knuckles cracked.

#

I was walking into my office when Celeste, my PA, motioned me over. 'There's someone here to see you,' she said in a low voice. 'She wouldn't tell me who she is or what she wants. She says it's urgent.'

I looked over into the small waiting room. A young woman perched on the edge of an armchair, legs pressed neatly together and hands in her lap. Her long dark hair was messy, not in a fashionable way, but as if she'd just got out of bed. Her eyes, brown and deep-set, held my gaze; the look in them saying, 'I won't take no for an answer.'

Occasionally I had women try to see me to ask for a job or to sell me something, thinking that if they went straight to the boss, they'd have more of a chance. It never worked, of course. But this woman didn't look like a businesswoman; she was dressed in jeans and jacket and flat shoes. And although she was sitting perfectly still, I sensed she was nervous.

I'll admit it would have been easier to send her away if she was plain, but she was striking in a way I couldn't describe. And I was curious.

I gestured to her. 'Come in, Ms. ...'

'Frida.'

I opened my office door and stood aside as she entered, handbag over her shoulder. She was thin, the tight jeans emphasising her lack of curves. I sat at my desk and she sat in the chair opposite, hugging her handbag to her chest. It was good quality leather.

'What can I do for you, Frida?'

'I'm your daughter.'

Whoa! I hadn't seen that one coming. 'I'm sorry, you're mistaken. I don't have a daughter.'

Frida opened her handbag, rummaged around in it and drew out a crumpled piece of paper. She handed it to me. It was a birth certificate. Frida Joan Shipp, born 6th June 1997 at Liverpool Hospital, Sydney. Mother: Carol May Shipp. Occupation: Artist. Age: 22. Father: Jack Arthur Forbes.

Occupation: Labourer. Age: 24.

That was my name, except for the Jack instead of Jackson. And I had lived with Carol Shipp for a couple of years in my early twenties. I checked Frida's date of birth again.

She was 21. When did I leave Carol to move to Melbourne? It was before 6 June 1997, but how long before, I couldn't remember.

Frida was watching me, leaning forward, her shoulders tense. I handed her back the birth certificate. 'That means nothing. Carol could have put anyone's name on it.'

She rummaged around inside her handbag again, drew out another piece of crumpled paper and handed it to me. It was a charcoal sketch, a side on portrait of a man staring into the distance. Stubble on his chin and a cigarette dangling from the corner of his mouth. I knew it was me and that it was Carol's artwork even before I saw her signature at the bottom of the page. She'd made me look more glamorous than I was, had given me an enigmatic Humphrey Bogart air. I couldn't remember her drawing it—we were both probably off our faces.

I handed the drawing back to her. 'It still doesn't prove anything. Not meaning any disrespect to your mother, but Carol wasn't fussy about who she slept with.' Especially when she needed money for drugs. None of us were, to be fair. We were young, and this was the 90s—grunge, share houses, share drugs, share women.

'I know you're my father.' Her brittle tone failed to hide her desperation. 'Ever since I can remember, my mother told me you were dead. Then about six months ago she admitted she'd lied to me. She said she didn't know where you were, but it was quite possible you were still alive.'

'Why did she tell you I was dead?'

'She was angry at you for leaving her; you were the only guy she'd been with who hadn't beat her up or raped her. She said she didn't want me wasting my time trying to find you, that you didn't deserve to have a daughter.'

It was true that Carol hadn't wanted me to go to Melbourne. She begged me to stay. I asked her to come with me, but she refused. All her friends were in Sydney, that's where the art scene was happening. She'd had paintings in a couple of exhibitions. If she could just keep her shit together and stay off the drugs she could make a go of it.

But I knew that if I didn't leave, I'd never get my head straight. She must have found out she was pregnant after I left; if she'd known beforehand, she'd have used it as a lever to persuade me to stay. It was convenient for her to put my name on the birth certificate, I wasn't there to protest and would be none the wiser.

Could Frida possibly be my daughter? She had the same shaped face as me, long and angular, and I also had brown eyes and dark hair, now streaked with grey. She certainly didn't take after her mother who was fair-haired, with large, pale eyes that always had a startled, anxious look about them.

'How did you find me?' I asked.

'It was hard at first, because I was looking for Jack Forbes. Do you know how many Jack Forbses there are in this country? Mum said you'd gone to Melbourne but you could have been anywhere by now. Then on the internet I saw a newspaper article about Jackson Forbes, some charity you were involved with, and I wondered if Jack was short for Jackson. Then I looked on LinkedIn and found your date of birth and it matched. As soon as I saw your photo I knew you were my father.'

I had to admit, her story made sense. Carole had only ever known me as Jack; I'd never told her it was short for Jackson, because I hated the name. When I moved to Melbourne, I resurrected Jackson as a way of separating my old life from my new.

'Frida, you may well be my daughter. I'm not denying that. But I need to know for sure. The only way to do that is to have a DNA test.'

'There's no time for a DNA test. I need your help now.'

Here we go. The sob story about needing money.

'What sort of help?'

'I have…' She took in a breath and swallowed. 'I killed a man. He was about to rape me so I shot him and now Teff McGill is after me and probably the cops as well.'

'You shot a man?'

I've always considered myself a good judge of character. It comes from having lived on the edge; that survival instinct has never left me. If you'd asked me ten minutes earlier if this girl was capable of killing anyone, I'd have scoffed.

'And why is Teff McGill after you?'

Teff McGill was a notorious crime boss, one of the few who'd escaped the Melbourne Gangland Wars in one piece. He was often in the news, usually to do with allegations of serious drug offences that never seemed to come to anything. Hence the nickname Teff, short for Teflon—nothing stuck to him.

'Because the man I killed was one of his heavies.'

'Jesus.' If she was involved in some way with McGill, I didn't want to know any more.

'Even if what you're telling me is true, there's no way I can help you.'

Frida opened her handbag again, whipped out a pistol and aimed it at my chest. 'You have to help me.'

Instantly I broke out in a sweat; my mind jumping back to the last time I'd had a gun pointed at me. Frida's hand trembled almost imperceptibly, but there was a determined set to her jaw. She shot a man in self-defence, but was she capable of shooting someone in cold blood? I doubted it, but then my judgment about her not being a killer had been incorrect.

'Put the gun away. I can't help you if you kill me.'

She slowly lowered the pistol, but kept it in her hand, resting it on her handbag.

'I have a board meeting after lunch and I'd like to talk to Carol. Give me her phone number.'

I pushed a pen and piece of paper over to Frida. She wrote down a phone number and handed the paper back to me.

'How is she, anyway?' I asked.

Frida's eyes flashed. 'What the hell do you care?'

'Don't give me that bullshit, there are reasons I left that neither you nor Carol are aware of.'

Frida shrugged. 'She's okay. She does really well with her art until she gets on the drugs and then she's hopeless. She's been in and out of psychiatric hospitals for the last few years.'

'She still into the smack?'

She nodded. 'I think the mental problems have more to do with the acid.'

We all did acid now and then, but Carol must have really got into it after I left. She always said she did her best paintings when she was on a trip. If Frida was hanging out with Teff McGill's crowd, it was more than likely she was doing drugs herself. Apart from her thinness, though, she didn't have the appearance of an addict. Her hair was glossy and her skin and eyes were clear.

'There's a hotel two doors up, The Regency. I'll meet you there in the lounge bar at five o'clock.'

She looked at me warily; I could see she was thinking that I wouldn't turn up and this was my way getting rid of her.

'I promise I'll be there,' I said.

'I need money. I've been on the run for the last three days and I've used all my cash. I haven't eaten since yesterday.'

I took out my wallet, slipped out a fifty dollar note and handed it to her. I was half-expecting her to wave the pistol at me again and demand that I give her all my cash. But she put the note and the pistol in her handbag and stood up, with the sulky look of a child who's been told to run along and play because the grown-ups want to talk about adult things.

If she disappeared I was only down fifty bucks. But something told me she wouldn't.

CHAPTER TWO

I rang the mobile number Frida had given me for her mother, but it rang out and went to message bank. I didn't leave a message, in case Carol didn't want to talk to me and blocked my call next time I rang. Surely she couldn't still be angry with me after all these years, but I wasn't taking any chances.

In the board meeting, I found it difficult to concentrate on the matters being discussed; my mind was still replaying Frida's visit.

'What's your take on this, Jack?' Keith Anderson, the senior operations manager, asked me. He leaned back in his chair, his hands clasped over his paunch.

I remembered we were discussing increasing the budget of the sales and marketing department, so they could hold conferences on eco-friendly packaging and develop a higher profile in this field.

'Sounds fine to me, I'm all for it.'

I pretended not to notice the looks and raised eyebrows Keith exchanged with the other board members. Usually I was the one who insisted that we thoroughly examine any requests to increase departmental budgets to keep everyone honest.

'I'm really pleased to see that we're all on the same page,' Oliver said. In his Hugo Boss business suit, he looked the part of the head of Sales and Marketing, but he had one of those bland faces you forgot the minute he walked out of the room. If you typed 'young businessman' into Google images, he'd be there.

'As you've read in the report,' he gestured to the 50 page laminated and bound reports we each had in front of us, and which I'd only skimmed through to see if there were any sexy bits, 'we've come up with a strategic plan to leverage the company as a thought leader in our core business, particularly in environmentally-friendly packaging, which is the most important issue for us to address going forward.'

I glanced around the table at the five other board members and half dozen senior executives. If they thought it sounded like a load of bullshit, they weren't letting on. If someone could come up with a strategic plan to speak and write plain English, Palmer Products Packaging would have an even better chance of becoming a thought leader, whatever that was.

After more discussion on brand alignment during which I zoned out, Ron Viertel, the Chairman of the Board, thanked Oliver for his enlightening presentation, and Oliver packed his briefcase and left. We voted unanimously for a 25% increase in funding. Oliver had put the case for a 50% increase, but departments always requested more than they thought they would get. Lindsay would be happy, anyway. As creative director of Sales and Marketing, she had contributed a lot of the ideas in Oliver's report.

After the meeting we usually adjourned to our own bar in the next room for a couple of whiskeys. I excused myself, saying I had another urgent meeting and left before anyone could ask questions.

I went back to my office, closed the door and dialled Carol's mobile number. It had almost rung out when a voice answered, 'Hello.' Soft and wary.

'Carol, it's Jack.'

Silence.

'Jack Forbes.'

'Jack?' Her tone was high in disbelief.

'How are you, Carol?'

'I'm okay. Why are you calling?'

'A young lady has turned up in my office claiming to be my daughter.'

'Frida's there? She found you?'

'Yes. She showed me her birth certificate, but I want to confirm it with you. You know how it was back then. How can I be sure she's really my daughter?'

'Look at her, Jack. She looks nothing like me.'

'I wasn't the only dark-haired brown-eyed guy around.'

'I swear to you, she's yours. I can even tell you when she was conceived. Remember when we went to the farm to dry out?'

How could I forget it? It was the turning point of my life. I'd made the decision to get off drugs and out of crime. My mate Carl Mooney had a cousin, Tom, who owned a dairy farm on the Central Coast of New South Wales. Tom would be happy for me to stay there to dry out and get well— free board in exchange for helping him on the farm. Carl had gone there himself once to get off drugs—not that it did him any good.

I persuaded Carol to come with me; in truth she needed it more than I. I was heavily into pot, but only a social user of hard drugs. She had a daily heroin habit, and had a lot worse time of it than I did. She spent the first ten days in bed or on the toilet, shivering and shaking uncontrollably. We got well with good food, fresh air and hard physical work.

After we'd been there for six weeks and I felt more alive than I could remember feeling in my whole life, I decided to move to Melbourne. When Carol refused to come with me, I just up and left, going straight there from the farm. I didn't even bother going back to our flat in Sydney to collect the rest of my stuff. I knew if I went back, I might never leave.

'Of course I remember it.'

'It was then, after we both got better.'

I remembered that too. We were both clear-headed, as if our minds had been spring-cleaned, with energy to burn, making love like rabbits. Tom caught us at it once in the tool shed when we were supposed to be tidying it. 'Oops, sorry,' he said, closing the door in a hurry.

'I knew pretty soon after I got back to Sydney that I was pregnant. I had real bad morning sickness, but I stayed off the drugs all through my pregnancy. She's beautiful, isn't she, Jack? Don't you think she's beautiful?'

'Yes, she is.'

'I named her after Frida Kahlo.'

Of course. Frida Kahlo was one of Carol's favourite artists.

'Why did you tell her I was dead?'

'It was better for her. Centrelink tried to track you down to pay child support but when they couldn't find you, it was easier to pretend you were dead. I didn't want her trying to find you, and then being upset if you didn't want to have anything to do with her.'

'Frida says it was because you were angry at me for leaving you.'

'I was for a long time, but I see now why you did. You needed to get away from everything, including me.'

Deep down I was glad Carol had refused to come with me to Melbourne. I knew it would be hard for her to stay off drugs and she'd either drag me down with her, or I'd feel responsible for her and obligated to help her, a stress I didn't need when trying to make a new life.

'I'd been thinking to myself for a long time that I should tell her you weren't dead, but I couldn't seem to find the courage. Then one day she came to visit me in the psych ward; they had me doped up on something and I didn't know what I was saying and I just blurted it out. But I'm glad she knows now. Is she all right?'

'She's fine.' Carol didn't need to know that Frida was in trouble. From what Frida had told me, she had enough on her plate.

'How about you Jack, have you been going all right?'

'Yes, I'm fine.'

"Are you married? Do you have kids?"

'Married, yes. Kids, no.'

I cut her off abruptly, not wanting to discuss my personal life with her. 'It was good to talk to you, Carol, but I have to go.'

'Of course. You and Frida have a lot of catching up to do.'

I was about to ring off when Carol said, 'Has Frida told you much about me?'

'A little,' I said cautiously.

'I was going really good, I was clean. I had a real nice public housing flat, had done some exhibitions and sold a few paintings.' Her voice shook. 'And then this artist I was hanging around with got back into the smack and I did too and it all went to shit after that. I got behind in the rent and lost the flat, then I ended up in the psych hospital and now I'm in this shitty old boarding house full of stinking old men.'

She was sniffling into the phone. 'I've got nothing, I even hocked all my art stuff.'

I tried to muster some sympathy. 'I'm very sorry it hasn't worked out for you.'

'Don't feel sorry for me, I'm a survivor. I've started over again before. At least Frida's not like me, she's got a great job in marketing, earns good money and has a lovely apartment on the beach. And she dresses nice and goes out to dinner and all. She's beautiful, isn't she?'

'Yes, she is. I really have to go. Are you sure you're okay?'

'I'm fine, really I am. Give Frida a big hug from me and tell her to visit me soon.'

#

I entered the lounge bar of The Regency and spotted Frida sitting at a corner table. She was hunched over a magazine with an empty champagne glass in front of her. Her neck was bare, her hair pulled up under a cap.

She looked up. There was relief in her eyes as she watched me approach. I remembered that some of the Board members often came to this bar to continue the post-meeting drinking. I didn't want any rumours going around about me being seen with a young woman.

'Come on,' I said, 'there's another pub further down the street I'd rather go to.'

She followed me outside and walked beside me down the street along the Yarra River. When I first moved to Melbourne, I thought the Yarra River was just brown. But now that I had an office that overlooked it, I realised there were many shades of 'just brown.' Today it was the colour of muddy coffee.

I swore to myself as we bowed our heads against the wind. The sun had been high and bright in the sky this morning; now the wind was whipping around me as if it had a personal vendetta against me. I never got used to the four seasons in one day. Everyone warns you about it and it's a cliché description of Melbourne, but it's true. It was almost summer, for God's sake, and everyone was huddled into overcoats. The faces of the commuters hurrying to catch their trains and buses home were as grey as the sky.

Frida wore only a T-shirt under her jacket, and was hugging herself as she walked. I took off my coat and held it out to her. She shook her head, not missing a stride.

'You look frozen,' I said.

'I'm okay.'

I shrugged and put my coat back on. She'd just demanded at gunpoint that I save her life, fleeced me for $50 and was now refusing my offer of a coat. Was she trying to be a martyr? Maybe she needed to be the one in control. We arrived at the Settlers Inn, a cosy wood-panelled bar overlooking the Yarra. As I opened the door, the heat wrapped itself around us like a warm blanket.

I found us a table away from the crowd and went to the bar to get our drinks—champagne for Frida and a light beer for me. I got the impression she wasn't just drinking champagne because I was paying; she ordered it confidently and without hesitation, as if it were her usual tipple.

'So what made you move to this Godforsaken city?' I asked her as I placed the drinks on the table.

'My boyfriend moved here. I was 16, school was crap, so I came down to join him. Then we split up and by that time, I kind of liked it, so I decided to stay. I wanted to make a fresh start. Like you.'

How much had Carol told her about my past? I'd follow that up later.

'I spoke to your mother a few minutes ago.'

Her expression was wary, but curious. '"Did she convince you that I'm your daughter?'

'It seems more than likely that you are.'

Frida looked at me uncertainly, as if not sure how I was going to react.

'This will take me some time to get used to.'

Getting used to a daughter coming to me fully formed, never having held her as a baby, squirming in my arms, clapping as she took her first wobbly steps, teaching her to throw a ball and ride a bike, weathering the turbulent teenage years as I picked her up from parties and checked out her boyfriends.

I had the strange sensation of being in a play with no script, floundering around for words and feelings. I felt no emotion for the woman in front of me. She was my daughter; I could accept that in my mind but my heart hadn't caught up.

'Do you have any other kids?' Frida asked.

'No.'

Now was not the time to mention our six failed IVF attempts and our decision to give up before we both went stir crazy. How would Lindsay feel now with me turning up on the doorstep with a daughter from the past? I had an inkling she wouldn't welcome it.

'Your mum was telling me all about your fantastic marketing job. Sounds almost too good to be true.'

Frida said nothing, fixing her attention on a noisy group at a nearby table.

"You made that up, didn't you, to make your mother happy. Here's what I think. If you're hanging around with Teff McGill's cronies, the only marketing you're doing is drugs.'

She met my gaze. 'So what? You're hardly in a position to criticise me. You did plenty of it, from what Mum tells me.'

'I'm not criticising you, just asking a question. What exactly do you do for Teff?'

Frida glanced around her. The hubbub of conversation was loud; no one was giving us a second glance. 'I'm a courier,' she said in a low voice. 'After a shipment comes in, I do his drops for him around the city. It's good money. I have a great apartment near the beach, nice clothes and I can afford to go out to good restaurants and eat and drink what I like. The last thing I wanted to do when I left home was to live like Mum.'

'Your swanky lifestyle is worth nothing to you now.'

'How could I know that pig would try to rape me? That could happen to anyone any time.'

'What exactly happened?'

The muscles in her neck tensed. She picked up her glass and downed the rest of her champagne in one gulp.

'You want another?'

She nodded. I went to the bar and got us both another drink. When I returned, she took another sip of the champagne, then gripped the stem of the glass with both hands. 'I was doing a drop-off at one of the fitness centres Darcy owns—owned, and he lured me into his office on the pretext of showing me his renovation plans for the gym. He grabbed me and threw me on the ground and started ripping off my jeans. I managed to knee him in the balls, which gave me enough time to get my gun out of my coat pocket. I didn't intend to kill him, I was just going to threaten him. Then he came lunging at me to get the gun, so I pulled the trigger. I didn't stop to think, it was me or him.'

'Did you tell Teff?'

'It wouldn't make any difference. He's big on loyalty. He and Darcy had been best mates since they were kids. I heard that Darcy even took the rap for him and did jail time.'

'More fool him. Where was the fitness centre?'

'Clayborne.'

Clayborne was one of the outer rural suburbs, a popular destination for cashed up tree-changers. I took out my smartphone, Googled 'Murder Darcy Clayborne' and found an online newspaper report from the previous day.

'Police are investigating the murder of Darcy Bede, the owner of the national GetFit chain of fitness centres, at his Clayborne gym yesterday. Mr Bede, 48, was found on the floor of his office with a bullet wound to his chest. Police are seeking a slim, dark-haired woman in her early twenties, last seen wearing black jeans and a grey jacket, who may be able to help them with their enquiries. Anyone with any information is urged to call Crimestoppers.'

I handed it to Frida and watched her as she read it, biting her lip.

'At least you're not wearing the same clothes, and slim, dark-haired women in their early twenties are a dime a dozen.'

'I was too scared to go home. I went to Kmart and bought new gear. Not my style, but...' she shrugged.

'Is that gun you waved at me the same one you used on Darcy?'

'Of course not, I'm not that stupid. I buried it where no one will find it.'

'So you just happened to have a spare gun lying around?'

'I broke into my ex-boyfriend's house and took his.'

'So he's going to guess it was you who took it?'

'Maybe. But he's gotta find me.'

I took the phone back from her. 'I still don't see how I can help you.'

'There are two ways.' She reached into her handbag, took out a piece of notebook paper and handed it to me. It had a name on it, Jimmy, and a mobile number.

'Jimmy is the contact for a guy who does false passports. It usually takes a few days. I need a new identity so I can get out of the country. And I need somewhere to hide until the passport is done.'

'Whoa, let's go back a few steps. What's the worst case scenario here? That the cops somehow get enough proof to charge you? You killed him in self-defence, so you do a few years for manslaughter. Plus being in jail gets you out of McGill's clutches. Isn't that better than spending the rest of your life looking over your shoulder?'

'I don't care about the cops or jail. The worst case scenario is Teff. My being in jail won't stop him getting revenge, he's got spies everywhere. If he doesn't get to me while I'm inside, he'll be waiting for me when I get out.'

'Why can't you go to this passport guy?'

'Because the word would get back to Teff. It has to be someone they don't know.'

'Jesus, Frida, do you know what you're asking? You're asking me to do something criminal. And don't make any snide remarks about what I used to do. I'm not that person any more. What if someone finds out what I've done? There goes my job, my reputation, maybe my freedom. And what if Teff finds out I've helped you? He'll be after me as well.'

Tears welled up in her eyes. 'You're the only chance I've got of getting out of this country alive.'

I shook my head. 'I can't possibly make up my mind now. I need some time to think about it.'

Her face hardened in an instant. 'You're forgetting I still have the gun.'

'And you're forgetting I object to being threatened by my own fucking daughter.'

We glared at each other, the crescendo of chatter around us filling the silence between us.

'So I take it you have nowhere to stay tonight,' I said finally.

I took her silence as an affirmative.

'What would you have done if I hadn't been in the office today? If I'd been away?'

'Found a tree or a park bench. It wouldn't be the first time.'

I raised my eyebrows.

'Mum and I slept out a few times, in between houses.'

Jesus, Carol, how could you drag your daughter down with you? What life is that for a child, sleeping rough, surrounded by drunks and addicts and violence?

'I mean, about getting out of the country.'

'Nothing. I meant it when I said you're my last hope. It's a case of who finds me first—Teff or the cops.'

I picked up my phone from the table, opened Google and typed Teff McGill into the search bar. The top entry on Google was 'Non-Stick Charges for Teff McGill,' an entry from The Daily Telegraph a couple of years ago.

'Notorious criminal Terrence McGill has once again lived up to his nickname Teff, short for teflon. He walked free today from the Melbourne Magistrates Court after two counts of trafficking dangerous drugs and three counts of supplying dangerous drugs were dismissed, with the prosecution having no evidence to offer.

'Flanked by his legal team, including well-known criminal barrister Charles Porteous, McGill declined to comment as he left the courthouse. Mr Porteous also refused to comment, except to say, "My client is innocent, so justice has been done."

'McGill, who is rumoured to be linked to one of the world's deadliest gangs, the Mara Salvatrucha, has so far avoided any lengthy jail terms.'

Which was about as much as you could say without accusing him of bribery and corruption to stay out of jail. Having trafficking and supplying charges dismissed was no mean feat—the police weren't in the habit of laying such charges without sufficient evidence.

I hadn't heard of the Mara Salvatrucha, but just the name was enough to conjure up visions of the sort of gangsters who would chop off your feet and throw you in the river if you dared say a word against them. I studied the mugshot of Teff accompanying the article. Narrow face, large, hooked nose and a thin slash of a mouth. His expression was one of amused resignation, as if he were saying to the photographer, 'Come on, let's get this over with. We've both got better things to do.'

'You certainly picked the wrong person to piss off,' I said. If you want to play with the big boys you can't come crying when things go wrong. It was on the tip of my tongue to say it, but I refrained. 'I'm not making any promises about the passport, but I'll find you somewhere to stay. Not with me, though. If anything goes down, I don't want him or any of his associates anywhere near my home.'

'But nobody knows of my connection with you. Except for Mum, of course.'

'I don't want to risk it and in any case, my wife wouldn't be too impressed with you turning up out of the blue.'

Frida gave me a look that said she wasn't impressed with my wife not being impressed. The champagne had given her face a rosy sheen that highlighted the pucker between her eyebrows and the downward curve of her mouth. Did she always look so sulky or was that just for my benefit?

'I could put you up in a hotel.' There was nowhere else. I couldn't ask any of my mates to accommodate her and put them at risk. And I could hardly tell them the truth about Frida.

She shook her head. 'Too easy for the cops to find me. And Teff. Wherever there are people, someone will blab. It has to be somewhere off the beaten track.'

I stood up. 'I'm going to the Gents.'

'Jesus f... Christ,' I muttered underneath my breath as I stood at the urinal, ignoring the glance of the man beside me. So my brand-new daughter whom I didn't even know I had until today was now demanding that I consort with a criminal, get a false passport, and harbour a police suspect, when I hadn't done anything criminal for 21 years. And then she had the cheek to dictate where she was, or wasn't, going to stay. She could just damn well find her own place—I'd give her some money and send her packing. By her own accounts she'd done okay without me until now.

As I came out of the Gents, I glanced over at our table. Frida wasn't alone. A man was sitting opposite her, in my chair. He was wearing a suit, his back to me, leaning towards her and gesturing with his hands as he talked. Frida's reaction was obvious even from where I was standing—she was leaning back in her chair, her body emanating 'piss off' vibes, her hand clutching her champagne glass as if she were about to throw it in his face.

In a few strides I was at the table, towering over the man. He turned out to be a clean-cut boy who barely looked old enough to be of drinking age. He stopped mid-sentence, looked up at me and scrambled out of his chair.

'Sorry, was I in your seat?' he said. 'I was just introducing myself to your. …' He looked from me to Frida, struggling to define our relationship. 'Anyway, see you round.' He waved to Frida and made his way to the bar with the studied gait of someone who is trying hard not to appear drunk.

'You okay?' I said.

Frida gave a dismissive nod. 'I would have told him to fuck off but I thought he might get angry and I didn't want to draw attention to myself. Guys think if a girl's sitting by herself she must be hot for it.'

That much hasn't changed since I was her age. So much for Women's Lib. I took my seat again and said without preamble, 'My company has a warehouse in an industrial estate in Oakleigh, about half an hour's drive from here. It's closed down because we've moved to another premises and we haven't decided what to do with it yet. It's empty, so you can stay there for the time being. It will be cold and uncomfortable, but no-one will find you there.'

For the first time in the seven hours I'd known her, Frida looked hopeful. 'When can we go?'

'Right now, if you like.'

CHAPTER THREE

The front doors of Yarra Towers were still open; they weren't locked until 7 p.m. We went down to the basement car park, I unlocked my car and Frida slid into the passenger seat.

'I have to get the warehouse keys from my office,' I said. I took the elevator to the 12th floor, unlocked the front door of Palmer Packaging Products and went in.

The office was deserted, except for a light under the closed office door of Hugh Morrison, the Chief Financial Officer. He was probably working on another of his interminable risk analysis reports.

I went to my office and retrieved the warehouse keys from my desk drawer. On my way out, I heard muffled voices and a woman's giggle coming from Hugh's office. A giggle that I recognised, although I hadn't heard it for a long time.

I stopped in my tracks outside the door. A man's low voice, then another giggle and a female's soft voice. Rustling noises, a thump and a gasp, then another giggle. I'd heard enough. I continued on my way out of the office, down in the elevator and to the car. The second shock within 24 hours—could my day possibly get any worse?

I was silent as we crawled through the commuter traffic to Oakleigh. Frida slumped in her seat, her cap over her face, hugging her handbag to chest. The incident in the office replayed itself in my mind. My rational self tried to reason that it could have been another woman in Hugh's office, but I knew otherwise.

Lindsay's giggle was unmistakable; it was the first thing that had attracted me to her. While having a drink in an inner city bar with a mate, I'd heard it—low, throaty, mellow. I looked across to the table beside me; her appearance matched her giggle. Attractive and elegant in a way that denoted natural class, her short, stylishly-cut blonde hair emphasizing her cheekbones and full lips. She was with a group of women and I watched her, mesmerised, as she chatted and laughed, running her long fingers with their crimson manicured nails up and down her wine glass. She had an air of self-assurance that I found alluring and erotic; she would be the sort of woman who would let you know in no uncertain terms what she liked.

I walked over, charmed my way into the conversation and obtained her phone number. When I phoned her and she jumped at my suggestion of a motor bike ride and a picnic for our first date, I was already smitten. And my assumption about her assertiveness in bed was proved correct.

But why Hugh? Or could it have been someone else with Lindsay in his office? I dismissed that idea—Hugh didn't like people in his office when he wasn't there (it made me wonder if he had a secret porno stash) and always made a point of locking it before he went home. Lindsay and I used to joke about his mannerisms—the feminine swing of his hips as he walked, the way his eye twitched when someone disagreed with him, his obsequious charm in the presence of women—the more attractive they were, the smarmier he was. When did she stop laughing at him and start wanting to fuck him?

I heard a delicate snore and glanced over to see Frida's head lolling against the window, her mouth open. She wouldn't have slept much over the last couple of days. I turned my thoughts to buying her some supplies for the night. Most of the stores we passed were closed, but I spotted an Aldi supermarket that was open and pulled in to the car park.

Frida jerked her head upright and looked around. 'Just doing some shopping,' I said. 'Be back shortly.'

I returned with two large shopping bags containing a sleeping bag, a foam rubber mat, blanket, pillow and torch and batteries, as the electricity to the warehouse had been cut off. 'Just a few essentials to keep you safe from cockroaches and rats,' I said. She shuddered.

A few kilometres on we came to a Hungry Jacks and I pulled in to the drive-through and ordered us a burger, fries and Coke each. I'd sent Lindsay a text message before we left the Settlers Inn that I'd be late home. She probably wasn't even home herself yet, depending on how long Hughie-boy could keep it up. I obliterated that image from my mind. The tantalising junk-food aroma filled the car as Frida wolfed her food down straight away. She was wiping her mouth with her napkin as we arrived at Summer Creek Industrial Park.

I drove down avenues of softly-lit concrete and glass buildings to our company warehouse at the end of a no-through road. It was one of the first buildings in the park and looked its age—a faded, red brick construction stained with patches of mould and moss. It was several stones' throw from its neighbour, also a disused warehouse, and backed on to scrubby bushland. An ideal spot to hide a fugitive.

Even though there was no-one around at this time of day, I parked at the back of the warehouse, so my car wasn't visible from the road. Darkness was closing in. I put the batteries in the new torch I'd bought and Frida held it as I unlocked the padlock on the back door. It opened with a groan and we stepped inside. I took the torch from Frida and shone it around. L-shaped, concrete floor with a high row of windows along each wall which didn't let in much light, even in the middle of summer. It was dank and cold and gloomy.

'Your room, Madame,' I said.

'It's kind of spooky.'

Our voices bounced back at us.

'You'll be fine. There are no ghosts, as far as I know. Let me give you a guided tour.'

I led her to the far end of the warehouse, the torch light bobbing in front of us, our footsteps echoing on the floor. Out of the corner of my eye, I saw what looked like a rat's tail disappearing into a hole in the wall, but thought it best not to mention it. 'This used to be a distribution centre for our cardboard boxes. It's only been empty for a few weeks, so it's reasonably clean.'

We rounded the corner to a small room. I pushed open the door and shone the torch over a grubby tiled floor, a stained toilet and cracked washbasin. A couple of fat cockroaches scuttled away behind the toilet. Frida flinched. The toilet paper hanger was empty and a cake of soap on the washbasin looked prehistoric. 'All mod cons, apart from toilet paper, which I forgot. I'll bring some tomorrow, and some new soap.'

We went back out to the car and retrieved the purchases from Aldi and my dinner. Once inside the warehouse again, I handed the bag to Frida.

'Sorry I've got no chocolates to put under the pillow.'

Frida unpacked the goods, laid out the foam mat and the pillow, unzipped the sleeping bag and slid into it, still fully dressed, draping the blanket over her shoulders. I placed the torch on the floor so it shone a pool of light in front of us, lowered myself on to the floor and got stuck into my dinner.

I offered Frida my fries; she shook her head. I pushed them in front of her.

'I've got dinner waiting for me at home,' I said. It was a lie, but it did the trick. I watched her long, slender fingers as she shovelled the fries into her mouth.

'Did you inherit your mother's artistic talent?'

She shook her head as she swallowed a mouthful. 'She wanted me to be an artist, she had this fantasy that we could open an art gallery and have a mother-daughter exhibition. She even sent me to art lessons, but it was pointless.' Her lip curled. 'My art teacher was gross. He had piggy eyes and a stomach that wobbled like a jelly and he was always forgetting to do up his fly. He tried to grope me once. I poked him in the eye with a paintbrush, took off and refused to go back.'

I laughed. 'Good for you. It must have been hard for you growing up with your mum the way she was.'

She shrugged. 'I didn't know any other life. Some days she'd be so out of it I'd have to get myself off to school. Every so often the neighbours would report her to Child Services and the officers would come round and give her a good talking to and she'd stay off the drugs for a while, until the next no-hoper junkie came around.

'We never stayed in the same place for more than six months because mum was always behind in the rent and we'd get evicted. I was always the new kid at school, so I didn't wait for the other kids to hate me. The first day I'd say, "I was the gang leader at my other school and if you want to be in my gang, line up here." They did, and I was always in trouble.'

'Your mum is very proud of you. She told me how beautiful you were at least half a dozen times.'

'No thanks to her.'

She finished the fries and wiped her hands on a paper napkin.

'Will you be all right?' I asked. 'I wasn't joking about the rats and cockroaches.'

She shuddered. 'Rats give me the creeps.'

'I'll bring some bait tomorrow.'

'I also need a packet of permanent blonde hair dye, hair cutting scissors, and a change of clothes.'

'What size are you?'

'Eight. A pair of jeans and a shirt will be fine.'

I finished my burger and Coke, picked up my food wrappings and stood up. 'I'll come by in the morning with all the stuff and bring some more food as well. Do you have a phone?'

'No, I got rid of it so the cops couldn't trace me.'

'Anything else you need?'

'A toothbrush and toothpaste, a cake of soap. And a towel.'

I got out my phone and made a list of all the things I needed to buy on my Notes app.

'I'll see you in the morning. You'll be safe here. I'll lock the door, no-one will be able to get in.'

Frida was shivering and her face had gone a sickly shade of pale.

'You don't look well,' I said, 'I think you might be suffering from shock.'

'It's not that bad here.'

'I mean, delayed shock from the Darcy incident.'

'I'm okay.'

'I'll stay for a while just to make sure.'

'I'm fine,' she snapped. 'Please just go.'

I made my way reluctantly to the door and was about to open it when I heard, 'Wait!'

I turned. Frida looked small and lost and helpless huddled into her blanket.

'What about phoning Jimmy?'

'We'll talk about it tomorrow.'

#

The house was in darkness when I arrived home. I hit the garage remote control and drove in. Lindsay's car space beside mine was empty. My prediction was correct. Or maybe it wasn't so much Hugh's stamina—maybe they were enjoying a long afterglow. Perhaps they'd fallen asleep on the desk, or the carpet, or wherever.

I showered, changed into an old tracksuit and returned to the garage. I had converted the far space of our three car garage into a workshop. I opened the door and switched on the light. Lindsay referred to it as shantytown—shelves along two walls crammed with every tool imaginable and planks of varying sizes propped against another, two benches forming an L shape, both covered in tools, nails, bits of wood, tins of varnish and paint and sandpaper. A fine layer of sawdust covered the concrete floor. In one corner stood two of my latest projects—a mahogany coffee table, shining darkly, with a built in magazine rack underneath and a rocking horse, complete with white mane and leather reins, waiting to be varnished.

I breathed in the aroma—pine, mahogany, cedar and sawdust, all mixed in an exotic, woody perfume. The tightness in my shoulders loosened and a sense of calm settled over me. On the nearest bench, my latest creation shone out of the surrounding mess—a red cedar jewellery box, a present for Lindsay for our wedding anniversary in a couple of weeks. It was in the design of a miniature cabinet—two long bottom drawers for larger items such as necklaces and two rows of three small drawers above, for smaller items such as rings and earrings. I'd inlaid each drawer with velvet and only had to attach the gold-plated handles, lying on the bench nearby, to complete it. A simple, classic design, something I knew would appeal to her taste and her decree that everything have its place.

I ran my fingers over its smooth surface. The brown-orange burnish of the wood glowed under the light, the pattern of dark knots like whorls of chocolate. Every hour I'd spent on it, I'd visualised Lindsay's face when I presented it to her—surprise, delight, love even. Expressions I hadn't seen for a long time.

My mind flashed back again to our first meeting. Lindsay told me later she'd been attracted to my 'shaggy good looks and knockabout charm.' I'd been straight for four years by then, labouring for Mort in his home renovation business. I told her about my past early on, and I think the 'bad boy' aspect added to my appeal.

It was apparent from the start that despite her privileged upbringing, Lindsay was down to earth, and our tastes were similar in superficial things like music and movies that you think are important at that age. And unlike other women I'd dated, she had a sense of adventure. She was up for anything I did—windsurfing, go-kart racing, and though she was scared of heights, she even went abseiling with me on a couple of occasions. She loved to ride pillion on my motorbike as we went for a Sunday outing to the Dandenong Ranges or the Mornington Peninsula. I only had a Yamaha Virago 500 then, the best I could afford, but I was proud of it. The first motor bike I owned that I hadn't stolen.

But the thing I loved doing most was making her laugh; watching her face light up like she'd swallowed the moon and was glowing from the inside. When I asked her to marry me and she said yes, I walked around for days with a huge grin that not even her father's disapproval could wipe off.

But good things don't last forever. The IVF changed us both. It turned Lindsay into a discontented shrew who took out all her fears and anxieties on me, and it turned me into an insensitive boor, who struggled to understand her almost obsessional desire to have children and couldn't give her the comfort and support she needed. Marriage started off bringing out the best in us and ended up revealing the worst.

But Hugh…

The distant purr of an engine became louder as a car pulled into the garage. A car door slammed, followed by the staccato clip of heels on the garage floor. I opened the door of the workshop. Lindsay swung around and put her hand to her heart in an exaggerated gesture.

'God, Jack, you scared the hell out of me!'

She'd done a good job of covering up the ravages of love-making. In her tailored pants and jacket and with her neat blonde bob and carefully applied make-up, she looked as immaculate as when she'd left the house this morning, exuding the demeanour of someone for whom fucking in the office after hours would be unthinkable.

She nodded her head in the direction of the workshop. 'What are you working on?'

It was an offhand question; she wasn't interested. She hadn't set foot in there for months, so I had no qualms about her discovering the jewellery box.

'Just a few bits and pieces. You're late,' I added, keeping my voice casual.

'I was having drinks with Louise. It's her birthday and Todd's away, so she was feeling lonely. I told you about it this morning.'

I had a vague recollection of her mentioning something about tonight as we were both rushing out the door. Her lips pursed in a moue of annoyance. I knew she was chalking up another fault to add to the list—I never listened to her.

A niggle of doubt crept into my mind. Could she be telling the truth? Why lie when it would be easy for me to check with Louise myself? Unless she'd forewarned Louise to cover for her. Or she was confident I wouldn't check.

'I'm going to have a shower.' She turned on her heel and went inside the house. Washing away the evidence? Ordinarily I wouldn't have thought twice about her having a shower the moment she walked in the door. I went back into the workshop, and fiddled around for a while, but couldn't muster the motivation to finish the jewellery box. I shut the door and went inside the house.

Lindsay was sitting in her robe on the couch in the living room, her bare feet on the footrest. Her head was bent over the iPad on her lap, a glass of wine in her hand. The TV was on; it was one of those cheesy reality shows. A guy with a toothy grin and a girl with huge breasts were holding hands and gazing into each other's eyes. Lindsay frequently brought work home and did it while watching TV, sometimes eating dinner at the same time. Multitasking she called it, but I don't believe there's any such thing. It was just a way of avoiding conversation.

'I found out today I have a daughter.' I imagined myself blurting it out. Just to see her reaction, to jerk her out of her own little world. To hurt her. Even though she'd never said so, I knew she blamed me for our inability to have children.

"Well, I got pregnant at 16,' she'd said, more than once. She had an abortion, but I knew what she meant—'At least I know I can get pregnant.'

Now I could say to her, 'It's not my fault, either.'

But I couldn't tell Lindsay about Frida and risk her telling others. And I couldn't swear her to secrecy without saying why.

I pulled up the sleeves of my tracksuit top and scratched at my arms. Today the itching had been particularly severe; my arms were red raw from my scratching. 'I'm going for a bike ride.'

Lindsay looked up. Bare of make-up, her complexion was sallow and there were bags under her eyes I hadn't noticed before.

'At this hour of the night?'

These days disapproval was her default tone of voice, as if she disapproved of my existence on this planet.

'I need to get some fresh air.'

I felt her eyes on me as I left the room. I changed into my Kevlar pants, jacket and boots, went into the garage and hauled out my GS1200 BMW bike. Back in the years when I was stealing motor bikes and taking them for joyrides, I'd never bothered to get a licence. When I went straight one of the first things I did was get a motorbike licence, vowing to myself that one day I would buy myself a top ride. It was one of the proudest moments of my life when I traded in my Yamaha for this beauty and wheeled it into my driveway, shining in all its proud, black glory.

I started her up, zoomed down the driveway and out onto the street. Soon I was out on the road heading towards the state park, the visor of my helmet up so I could feel the wind nipping at my face. The sky was an inky black vastness overhead, dotted with just the odd star. This was one of the reasons we'd moved to Warrandyte, a semi-rural suburb about 40 minutes from the

CBD—I wanted to be close to the country so I could get on my bike and escape. We also thought it an ideal area to bring up a family. Lindsay loved it at first—the tranquillity, the space, the clean air. But over the last few months she'd been complaining of the commuting time to the office, which never bothered her before, and browsing real estate sites for homes closer to the CBD.

I hammered the throttle and glided around the curves and twists of the rural road. Thoughts of Lindsay and Hugh floated away in the wind. It was how I imagined horse riding must be, to feel at one with the beast beneath you. This was my religion, good and clean and pure. Better than religion, sometimes better than sex. On the bike, I could be anyone—James Dean, Marlon Brando, Steve McQueen. Myself, even, the 'past' me with Carl Mooney, flying along the highway on our stolen motor bikes into the half bushland of Western Sydney, where we'd hoon about on the deserted roads.

The adrenalin would charge my body like an electric shock; the thrill of the crime and the danger of being caught was like a drug, but the most addictive sensation of all was one of freedom. For a couple of short hours, I was free from people, rules and judgment; I could forget the memories, fears and anxieties that skulked in the dark recesses of my mind. I knew that freedom was an illusion, but like a true addict, I craved it nonetheless. We'd abandon the bikes in the bush and jump the train home.

Ahead of me on the left was a park fronting the Yarra, the gums like tall shadowy ghosts in the dark. I pulled up beside a group of picnic tables. On weekends it was alive with families, dogs, balls, and frisbees. I dismounted and wandered down to the water's edge. The moon was high, a spotlight shining on the park, as if it were an empty stage. I fancied I could hear the echoes of children laughing and dogs barking in the whisperings of the trees. A lone owl hooted.

I picked up a small rock and threw it into the river. Plunk. Ripples spread outwards, then stillness. I picked up another rock and threw it in. Plunk. Ripples. Stillness. As a kid, I'd spent hours sitting on the bank of the creek at the end of our street throwing stones into the water, a simple mechanical activity that soothed me and put me in a trance, taking my mind off school and home and the mess of thoughts churning in my head. Sometimes Sam would join me and we'd skim stones across the water. His always went the furthest. He was better than I at everything. Except staying alive.

Everything you do causes ripples. Even doing nothing. I thought of Frida, alone in the warehouse, huddled inside the blanket, pale and shivering. I couldn't not do anything. Despite her stampeding into my life, demanding that I save her, not thinking or caring about the impact it would have on me. It wasn't my fault I hadn't been around as she was growing up, but at least I had a chance now to make up for it. What was the point of being a father if you couldn't help your daughter when her life was in danger? If I didn't help her, she'd be killed by Teff or one of his thugs, dead before I'd had the chance to get to know her. Or hunted down by the police and jailed for God knows how many years. Our only contact would be visits in the women's prison.

When I was 15 I'd accompanied a mate, Darren, to the women's correctional centre to visit his mother, who was jailed for manslaughter. She stabbed his father to death with a kitchen knife after he tried to strangle her. Darren hated going there, hated seeing what his mother had become and asked me to come for moral support. As we perched on the hard chairs in the prison visiting room under the watchful eyes of the screws, Darren's mother Vicki, a scrawny woman with a mouth downturned in permanent bitterness, kept up a non-stop monologue about prison life. It could have been a comedy routine if it weren't so tragic. Assault, stealing, bribery, rape, bullying, were all part of the fabric of daily life. If she crawled on to her bunk at night with her dignity and possessions intact, it was a good day. And good days were rare. No matter how tough Frida thought she was, I couldn't allow her to be subjected to that. Six months after her release from prison, Vicki died after overdosing on pills and alcohol.

The wind picked up and blew a bank of cloud over the moon. At once it was cold and black. I took my mobile phone out of my jacket pocket, turned on the torch and beamed my way back to the bike.

The trip home seemed faster—it always did—and as I parked in the garage, my cheeks still tingled from the night air. My limbs felt loose and relaxed and my itching had subsided to a dull tickle. I took off my helmet, hung it over the handlebars and went inside. Lindsay was still on the living room couch, hunched over her iPad. The wine glass on the side table was full again. I peered over her shoulder. She was on Facebook; so much for working. She quickly swiped out of the page and looked up at me.

'Did you have a nice ride?' Her tone of condescension made my gut boil and sullied all the goodness and cleanliness inside me.

'Why do you even pretend to give a fuck about what I do? And quit speaking to me as if I'm some lowly minion you keep around for someone to slag off at.'

I didn't wait for a reaction. I went into the bedroom, undressed and climbed into bed. I plugged my earphones into my phone and listened to my ocean waves app, these days the only way I could get to sleep. I was out to it by the time Lindsay came to bed.

CHAPTER FOUR

At 8 a.m. I phoned Celeste and asked her to reschedule my morning appointments. Then I went to my local camping goods store and bought a kerosene lamp, matches and a Thermos. Next stop was Kmart, where I bought Frida two pairs of long pants, a couple of shirts and some underwear. Not used to buying women's underwear, I had to take a blind guess at her bra size. I also picked up some rat poison, a pair of large scissors, blonde hair dye and shampoo, toilet paper and soap, a couple of towels, a toothbrush and a tube of toothpaste.

In the supermarket I bought a packet of muesli bars, some apples and bananas and a six pack of bottled water. On the way to the checkout I passed the stationery supplies and on impulse I threw in a sketch pad and a box of pencils. My final stop was the Vodafone store to buy a mobile phone and a month's worth of credit.

Back on the road, I called into McDonald's, ordered a plate of hot cakes for Frida's breakfast and smiling at the young assistant, persuaded her to fill the Thermos with coffee.

The industrial park was alive with its daily business as I drove past a variety of auto businesses, stationery supplies, hardware and a home brew store. I parked at the back of the warehouse, unlocked the padlock and opened the door. The room was dim, weak sunlight filtering in through the windows. Frida's sleeping bag and pillow lay in a rumpled heap on the floor, but there was no sign of her.

My heart leapt into my throat, until I realised she was probably in the bathroom. I went out to the car and hauled all my packages in. As I dumped them on the floor, Frida appeared from around the corner. Still pale, she didn't look much healthier than the previous night.

'How did you sleep?' I asked.

'All right until I heard a car in the middle of the night. It drove in, stopped, drove further on, came back again and drove out. It freaked me out, I couldn't go back to sleep after that.'

'That was probably security, they come by every now and then.'

I gestured to the parcels. 'All the birthday and Christmas presents I never gave you.' I handed her the pancakes and the Thermos. 'Have these while they're hot.'

I set out the rat pellets and cockroach baits around the perimeter of the warehouse, then sat on the floor checking my emails on my phone, watching Frida surreptitiously as she ate. She balanced the plastic plate on her lap, a curtain of dark hair hanging over her face, almost dipping into the maple syrup. I could see her as a little girl, in Barbie doll pyjamas, doing exactly the same thing. Did she ever have Barbie doll pyjamas? She looked up and caught me staring.

'What?'

'Nothing.' I took out the mobile phone I'd bought her, activated it and punched my mobile number into the contacts. 'This is for you to use just to call me. Any time, day or night.'

'What about your wife? Won't she get upset if I call you in the middle of the night?'

'I'll handle it. I hope you won't need to call me in the middle of the night.'

She wiped her mouth with her napkin. 'So, have you decided about calling Jimmy?'

'I'll do it on one condition. That you give me your gun.'

'Fuck off.'

'Suit yourself.'

'Why?'

'You're putting yourself in danger by having it. If the cops catch you, being in possession of a gun, even if it's not the one that killed Darcy, will only raise more questions and make it harder for you to plead your case. And if Teff finds you, my guess is you won't have a chance to use it.'

'What do you want with it anyway?'

'I'll throw it in the river where it can join the hundreds of other guns disposed of in there. I reckon the bottom of the Yarra must look like a weapons convention.'

Swearing under her breath, she reached into her handbag, took out the pistol and handed it to me. I slipped it into my coat pocket.

'Who is this Jimmy anyway? How do you know him?'

'He's a friend of a friend.'

Of course, isn't everybody in the criminal world?

'How does he forge the passports? They're high tech these days, with microchips.'

'He doesn't do it himself, he just passes on the information. There's a mole in the passport office who does them.'

Who would no doubt expect generous compensation for the huge risk he or she was taking.

'So exactly how much does it cost?'

'A few thousand. I'm not sure exactly how much."

'And of course you don't have that money.'

She didn't reply, but I knew the answer. Her money was probably spent as soon as she received it, on the trappings of her upmarket lifestyle she thought were so important.

'This is a very happy coincidence for you, isn't it?'

'What do you mean?'

'Not only did you find your long lost Dad just when you needed help, but he also happens to have a few dollars. I guess if I were just a factory worker you wouldn't want to know me.'

She gave me a look that would shrivel a grape into a raisin. 'How do you know what I'd want? You know nothing about me.'

I knew her better than she thought. Already she reminded me of myself at her age—the determined jut to her chin, the tilt of her head when she was thinking, the way she shied away from emotion. Her self-centredness and the arrogance of youth, knowing all the answers, thinking her way of life was superior to abiding by the rules and earning an honest living.

Frida rummaged in the bags I'd brought in and pulled out the sketch pad and box of pencils. 'Why did you buy these?'

'Thought you might like something to help you while away the long hours.'

'I told you, I'm hopeless at drawing. You may as well take them back and get a refund.'

She threw them on the ground and rummaged around in another bag, pulling out the towels, hair dye, shampoo and scissors.

'I need your help to cut and dye my hair.'

'If you trust me—I can't guarantee my workmanship.'

'I don't have a choice, do I? I can hardly go to a real hairdresser.'

I draped one of the towels around her shoulders and spread the other on the ground to catch the hair. She handed me her hair brush and I brushed her hair into a lustrous fall over her back. It was awkward, an intimate father-daughter moment that was out of place; had no history to bolster it.

I picked up the scissors. 'Here goes.'

I cut off her hair to just above the shoulders and watched it tumble on to the towel.

'How short would Madame like it?'

She twisted her arm around to feel where I'd cut it.

"A bit more off to collar length.'

I cut off more hair until it was level with the collar of her shirt, and snipped off as many of the loose ends as I could. It was awful, no shape to it, but if I tried to fix it, I'd make it worse.

'All done, Madame. I'm sorry I don't have a mirror so you can see what it looks like.'

'Probably for the best.'

I carefully picked up the towel from the ground and with Frida holding open an empty plastic shopping bag, I shook the hair into it. I slipped on the plastic gloves that came with the hair dye and following the instructions, applied the colour all over her hair with the brush.

'I'll be ready to open my own salon soon,' I said as I dabbed the last bit of dye on. I stood back and surveyed my handiwork. I was quite proud of it; slathering every hair with hair dye and getting none on her face had required a lot of manual dexterity.

Frida allowed herself a slight curve of her lips. 'Don't give up your day job.' While we waited the 20 minutes for the dye to take, she poured some of the coffee from the Thermos into the lid and offered me some. I shook my head.

'Where do you plan to go with your new passport and identity?' I said.

'I don't know yet. Somewhere that doesn't have an extradition treaty with Australia, in case the cops find me.'

'I hear Jamaica is very nice at this time of year,' I said.

'Jamaica would be good,' she said seriously.

'You realise you'll never be able to set foot in this country again?'

'Better than being in jail, or dead.'

I helped Frida to wash out the hair dye in the washbasin in the bathroom. There wasn't enough room for her to stick her head right under the tap, so I used the Thermos lid, filling it with water and pouring it over her head. Then I applied shampoo and conditioner and did a final rinse.

As Frida towelled her hair dry, I said, 'I have to go.' I had a queue of monthly reports from department heads in my email inbox waiting for my attention. 'I'll call in tonight. What do I say to this Jimmy character?'

'Tell him you want to buy some product, that's the code. He'll set up a meeting time.'

'How do you know you can trust him?'

She shrugged. 'I don't.'

'We're off to a great start, then.'

Taking the bag of hair rubbish with me, I unbolted the door, letting in a brief flash of sunlight before padlocking it again. I left the sketch pad and pencils where Frida had thrown them on the floor.

#

On my way to the office I pulled over at the first public phone box I saw. Using my mobile phone would alert Jimmy to my number and give him the opportunity to trace me. I dialled the phone number Frida had given me.

'Hello.'

'I want to order some product please."

'Ok, who's speaking?'

The tone was high-pitched and clipped.

'Carl.' It was the first name that popped into my head.

'Ok, Carl, what sort of product?'

This wasn't in the script. 'Some of your overseas products.'

'Who gave you this phone number?'

'A friend of a friend.'

Silence. Was he going to refuse? I half wished he would.

'I can't divulge their name,' I said.

'Ok, meet me tonight in the public bar at The Waterloo in St Kilda at six o'clock. If we decide to order it for you, it's ten thousand dollars. Five up front. Cash.'

He hung up in my ear. Ten thousand dollars! The mole in the passport office must be raking in a fortune. I made a mental note to myself to go to the bank before they closed; for that amount of cash, I'd have to request a withdrawal from the teller.

Once at work, I took advantage of Celeste being on the phone, waving to her and hurrying into my office before she could waylay me with messages. She gave me a quizzical look over her glasses. Although only in her twenties, she was wise beyond her years and I often imagined she could see right through me—that I was a fraud, projecting the demeanour of a successful businessman when in reality I was a criminal who hadn't let go of his past.

Frida's gun was burning a hole in my jacket pocket. I closed the office door, took it out and placed it at the back of my bottom drawer underneath a pile of papers. I'd get rid of it tonight on the way to the warehouse. I turned on my computer and while waiting for it to boot up, I stood at the window looking down over the Yarra.

The sun was shining today, turning the river into a ribbon of burnished golden brown. A steady stream of people hurried along the path beside the river. Even from twenty storeys up, they all looked to have a sense of purpose.

Was it real or were they just faking it, like me? I'd become a cliché, the man who busts his guts to get to the top to find out the view was not what he expected.

After I married Lindsay, she persuaded her father to employ me. I started off as a salesman and progressed through the ranks to national operations manager by sheer hard work, and I readily admit, a lot of charm. It was a proud moment when, after I'd been with the company for ten years, Don Palmer called me into his office. Haggard and yellow-faced from weeks of chemotherapy, he told me he was going to nominate me for managing director.

'I have the utmost confidence in leaving the business in your hands,' he said. His praise was a precious gift from a man not given to compliments. The Board voted me in two weeks before he died. As I sipped on my celebratory Scotch with the other Board members, I imagined my parents' reaction to my promotion.

'How many arses did you have to lick?' I heard my father's voice, ravaged from years of drinking and smoking, as if he were right beside me.

'That's nice, dear.' My mother, smiling at me through a Valium haze, whispering because if my father heard her praising me she'd cop a beating afterwards.

It made me glad they were dead. Sam would have been proud, though— he would have slapped me on the back and said,' Great work, bro.' And boasted about me to all his friends. An ache of loneliness stirred inside me.

I turned away from the window, sat at my computer and logged into my email account. Meeting invitations, reports to read, queries. Everything was always urgent, yet I knew that if I dropped dead right now sitting at my desk, the wheels of the business would churn on regardless.

Lately a yearning for something I couldn't identify had grown from a small niggle in the back of my mind to a persistent thrum of desire. For what? My attempts to assuage it—the hours idled away at the Crown Casino, the one night stands, flying along the highway at 120 kilometres per hour on my bike—were temporary diversions to camouflage the hollowness of my life. But instead they heightened it. If I were looking for a glib answer, I'd have said it was freedom I was looking for.

But freedom is an illusion. There are always limitations, external and internal, to our existence. And if I could free myself from my present life, where would I go and what would I do? And what about my marriage, or what was left of it? I was trapped in the life I'd built so diligently for myself, a victim of my own success. Perhaps the doctor was right; my incessant itching was due to stress.

The phone buzzed. 'Sorry to interrupt you,' Celeste said, 'but Hugh is wondering if you have time to see him.'

Hugh liked to have regular chats with me to discuss budgets and financial strategies. There was never any new information that we hadn't already discussed at meetings, and I realised long ago it was to make him feel important. Usually I made the time for him, because it amused me to listen to him. Now my first impulse was to tell him to get fucked.

But if I refused to see him today, he'd just keep persisting. 'Okay, send him in.'

The door opened and Hugh bustled in, in his usual flurry of self-importance, as if I were the one who requested the meeting and he had to make time in his busy schedule to see me. He opened the folder of papers he'd brought with him.

'Just wanted to check with you about a couple of the items we discussed at the departmental heads meeting, in particular the biodegradable packaging project.' He looked at me closely. 'Everything all right, Jack?'

'Fine. Fire away.'

I stared at him as he rambled on in his Oxford English voice, at his round cheeks, shapeless blob of a nose and turkey jowls. The more I tried to banish the image of him humping Lindsay on his desk, the more it persisted. One thing was for sure; her tastes had changed over the years. You couldn't find anyone less like a charming bad boy than Hugh. But Lindsay wasn't the person I married and I wasn't the man she married either.

A slow burn of anger was building up inside me. How dare he sit in front of me and prattle on as if nothing had happened when he was fucking my wife? The anger wasn't due to jealousy; it was the deceit that went with it.

Why didn't they just tell me from the start they wanted to be together and piss off? Or perhaps it was just a dalliance, a sexual thing and they had no intention of having a relationship. In which case I hardly had the right to take the high moral ground. But it didn't stop my wanting to ram Hugh up against the wall and punch that smarmy look off his face.

But this wasn't the time or place for confrontation. Or the person. Lindsay was the one I needed to confront.

CHAPTER FIVE

I was in the public bar of The Waterloo by 5.45 p.m. I needed something stronger than a beer, so I ordered a bourbon and took it over to a high table with two bar stools. The Waterloo had been a working-class pub renovated to attract the yuppies, and there was a mix of clientele from tradies to hipsters and businessmen. An ideal place in which to conduct shady business; no one would stand out.

I scanned the faces around me, trying to find a match with the voice on the phone. I had $5000 in hundred dollar notes stashed in a money belt under my shirt. I was wary of Jimmy's setup being a scam—expecting me to arrive with cash, and he and his associates (because he might not turn up alone) could somehow force me into a quiet corner, rob me and take off. At least the money wasn't so easily accessible where it was now, giving me time to foil them. How, I had no idea.

I felt a tap on my shoulder and turned around to see a Chinese man in a suit. Shortish, slight build, broad face. He gave me a radiant grin worthy of a toothpaste commercial.

'You're Carl.' The same clipped accent as on the phone.

'Yes.'

We shook hands. His grip was firm, belying his pale, delicate hands. I gave a surreptitious glance behind him.

'I am alone,' he said. He slid onto the stool across from me.

'Can I buy you a drink?' I asked.

'Okay, a soda water, thanks. I don't drink alcohol. It's the devil's poison.'

I'd already finished my devil's poison but decided against another. I needed a clear head. When I returned with the soda water, Jimmy nodded his thanks. He took a sip. 'Okay, what can I do for you, my friend?'

He knew what I was there for, and he knew that I knew he knew. 'I need a passport,' I said in a low voice, 'Not for me, for a friend.'

He studied me. His skin was waxy, as if he'd buffed and polished it. He could have been any age from his thirties to his fifties. I hoped to God he didn't recognise me. Not that there was anything noteworthy about me. The only time I'd ever been mentioned in the media was when I agreed to the company sponsoring the New Life program, and it was just a brief write-up on page three of the daily rag.

"So, do I pass the test?'

He grinned. 'I don't think you are a cop."

'How can you be so sure?'

'I have a sixth sense about police, especially when they're undercover.' He tapped his nose. 'They have a certain odour; I can smell them. You don't smell like one.'

'I'm glad to hear it.'

Jimmy put his hand in his pocket and drew out a mobile phone.

'Okay, is your friend male or female?'

'Female.'

'Do you have a photo of her?'

'No.'

Even if I had one, the last thing Frida would want was for her photo to be on Jimmy's records, despite her change of hair style.

'What does she look like?'

'In her 20s, thin, short blonde hair.'

Jimmy swiped his phone and tapped a few times. 'Pick the one that looks the most like her. But make sure you get the eyes right; they are the most important thing. They are the windows of the soul.'

He handed me his phone. The screen was full of mugshots of young female faces, all with short blonde hair—hundreds of them as I scrolled down. I finally chose a photo of a girl whose eyes were as close to Frida's as I could find. The face was a little fuller and the cheekbones not as pronounced as Frida's but it was close enough, given that passport photos are often not an accurate reproduction of what people look like in the flesh. It would certainly pass a cursory glance. I pointed to the photo as I handed the phone back to Jimmy. He tapped it and a tick appeared in the corner.

'Okay, do you have the money?'

'I do. I'll just be a few minutes.'

I made my way through the crowd to the Gents. There was no one behind me as I entered. Two men were standing at the urinal. I went into one of the stalls and reappeared a few minutes later after flushing the toilet. The cash was in an envelope in my inside jacket pocket, the money belt stuffed in my pants pocket. I washed my hands, exited and headed straight for my table, where Jimmy was waiting with a bemused smile.

'You take precautions, very sensible.' He nodded approvingly. I took the envelope from my pocket and handed it to him. He slipped it into his coat pocket.

'I trust that it's all there. If not, no passport.'

'How long will it take?'

'Okay, three business days. Meet me on Friday night at six o'clock at The Pink Elephant in Kew. With the rest of the money.'

'You get around, ' I said.

'I never do business in any place more than once.'

'You must see a lot of pubs.'

'It's not always pubs, but I see you are a man who likes a drink, so I'm happy to meet you in a pub.' He gulped down his soda water and slid off his stool. 'A pleasure doing business with you.'

We shook hands again. I watched him as he walked out the door and disappeared into the night.

#

Before leaving The Waterloo, I sent Lindsay a text message. 'Having dinner with a couple of mates at the Casino.' She knew I went there on occasions, and I'd led her to believe that I only had the occasional flutter. Whether she believed me or not, I didn't know. These days our lives rarely intersected; on weekends I was out on my bike, in the Casino or in my workshop and Lindsay was shopping, at the gym or on a social outing with her female friends.

On the outskirts of St Kilda, I headed to a secluded spot on the Yarra River I'd been to before. A woman I'd picked up at the Casino a few weeks ago had brought me back to her apartment. It was one block back from the river, behind a shopping centre and a small park. I figured there'd be few people, if anyone, there at night; I could pretend I was out for an evening stroll, then throw the gun in at an opportune moment.

I parked the car in the shopping centre carpark away from the other two cars. The only place still open was the Yum Tum Asian Takeaway, its garish lanterns swinging from the awnings. A man hurried out carrying three plastic bags of food, but didn't look my way as he got into his car. I walked over to the narrow pedestrian path skirting the river.

A fresh wind tugged at my jacket as I strolled along the path. I looked up at the apartment block, then quickly away. The woman (was it Suzanne? Something starting with S) lived on the top floor with river views, one of those modern apartments that was all glass. Even if she was looking down now, I was too far away to identify, unless she had binoculars. I tried to recall her face, but a mass of auburn hair and bee-sting lips was all I could picture. I wouldn't know her if I bumped into her in the street. She was an athletic lover and I had the impression she was trying to impress me with her moves.

Afterwards as we lay curled up together, I stared at the unfamiliar shapes in the darkness of the bedroom until she drifted off to sleep. Then I got up, dressed and left. No note, no goodbye. The usual stuff. And a false name and phone number so she couldn't track me down. The thrill was all in the risk, the anticipation.

I strolled along the path, both hands in my jacket pockets. I wrapped my right hand around the gun, which I'd wiped clear of fingerprints and placed in a plastic bag. A young couple walked towards me, arm in arm, too engrossed in each other to notice me. Two skateboarders thundered past me from behind. Baggy pants, backwards caps, a whiff of marijuana.

The Yarra was still and silent under the moonlight, a brackish odour filling the air. What secrets did it hide in its murky depths? Without missing a step, I pulled the plastic bag out of my pocket and gave it my best overarm shot. With a splash and a couple of ripples it disappeared. I continued walking. One more secret.

#

When I pulled up at the warehouse the moon had gone into hiding and darkness was descending. I got out of the car, hauling out the two bags on the seat beside me. One was full of books and magazines I'd taken from the bookcase in the living room before I left the house that morning. They were Lindsay's, but she wouldn't miss them. The other bag held a carton of Pad Thai I picked up from the Yum Tum Asian Takeaway after disposing of the gun. I waited for my eyes to adjust to the darkness before I unlocked the padlock and opened the door.

Inside, the kerosene lamp shone a pool of light onto the floor. Frida was huddled up in the sleeping bag with the rug on top. She sat up. I got a momentary shock to see her as a blonde. It looked peculiar with her dark eyebrows and made her pale complexion look washed out.

'Sorry to wake you.'

'I wasn't sleeping, just bored.'

I placed the bags on the floor beside her. 'Dinner and a few things to read which might alleviate the boredom.' The magazines were Home Beautiful and Vogue and the novels were romantic comedies—none of them probably to Frida's taste, but perhaps better than staring into space all day being ambushed by memories of her crime. The sketch pad and pencils were still lying on the floor where she'd thrown them, untouched.

Frida barely glanced at the bags. 'What happened with Jimmy?'

'All settled. I had to pick a photo. It's not as beautiful as you, but it'll do. I'm meeting him again on Friday night with the rest of the money and he'll hand over the passport.'

I didn't trust Jimmy. I still wasn't sure this wasn't a scam, and that I'd turn up at The Pink Elephant on Friday night to find no one there. There was nothing about him that I could put my finger on, maybe just an instinctive distrust of anyone in the criminal sphere. I smiled grimly to myself. Funny how I could think of criminals as 'them' when I was fast heading in that direction myself.

I certainly didn't trust Jimmy not to squeal if Teff or one of his heavies put the pressure on him to reveal information. If Teff were to find out about Frida's passport, the danger was no longer abstract, it was as real as the pinging of my nerve ends. And the question of whether I was willing to put my life in danger for a woman I believed to be my daughter was no longer abstract, either. I was already in it up to my eyeballs.

'Three days,' Frida said. 'A lot can happen in three days.'

'Time for us to get to know each other,' I said.

Frida's eyes blazed. 'Look, I appreciate what you're doing for me, but let's not do the father-daughter thing. Nothing you do or say can make up for the last twenty-one years.'

'Just a fucking minute, it's not my fault I didn't know of your existence.'

'And if you did know, would you have been a proper father to me?'

It was a question I'd posed to myself over the last couple of days. I liked to think that I'd have accepted the responsibility of fatherhood, even with the constraints of living 900 kilometres away. That I'd have visited Frida as often as I could and given Carol money to help with the expenses. But if I were truthful, I had to admit I was kidding myself. I may well have decided it would be too much of a risk and a burden on me, given that going straight meant cutting all ties with Carol and her lifestyle.

'To be honest, I don't know. But that's not the issue. You're blaming me for something that isn't my fault. I know you had it tough growing up with Carol but you're an adult now, so you can stop blaming her and start being responsible for your own life.'

I had an overwhelming desire to slap that expression off her face. I jammed my hands in my pockets and strode out.

#

As I got into the car my mobile phone beeped. Lindsay had replied to my text message. 'What about Hugh's birthday dinner??? We're at The Blue Duck.'

Shit. Lindsay had reminded me at breakfast, but it had slipped my mind after the events of the day. I wasn't in the mood for being social, especially with Hugh and his cronies. Could I make an excuse, a sudden illness?

But on second thoughts, going to the dinner would be a good opportunity to confirm Hugh and Lindsay's affair once and for all. From my observations it was impossible for two people in an illicit relationship to be in each other's presence and not give away some clue, no matter how subtle.

It was close to 9 p.m. by the time I arrived at The Blue Duck, an upmarket restaurant in Southbank in a lane crammed with restaurants and bars. The maître d' escorted me to the table. There were 12 altogether; Hugh and his wife Kate, a couple of Hugh's friends and their wives, his brother and sister and their partners. I'd met them all before, but didn't know any of them well. They were all pretty much in the Hugh mould, absorbed in their own importance. Kate, who as a journalist had a nose for bullshit and the cynicism to match, was the only person there I had any time for.

I made my apologies as I sat in the only empty chair next to Hugh. They were all on their main courses.

"Sorry, we couldn't wait,' Lindsay said. Her tone of voice was sub-zero degrees. 'But I guess you already had dinner at the Casino.'

'No worries, I'll just order a coffee.'

'I called into your office this morning, but Celeste said you rescheduled all your appointments and she didn't know where you were.'

Her tone was reproving. What was she accusing me of? Having a morning rendezvous? No one looked at me, all eyes on their meals.

'I went for a long walk, I needed some exercise.'

Hugh patted his stomach. 'I should be doing that myself.'

'Especially now you're 45,' Kate said. 'You're no spring chicken.'

She sounded narky; maybe they'd had a fight. A waiter in a bow tie hurried over and handed me a menu.

'I've already eaten, just an espresso, thanks.'

'Yes, sir.' A slight twitch of his lip was the only evidence of his displeasure at my turning up to his restaurant when I'd already eaten. In reality I was famished, and tried not to look at Hugh as he tucked into a huge rack of pork ribs with garlic mash.

The conversation flowed as freely as the alcohol. The usual topics—the property market, company tax laws, skiing holidays and of course, Aussie Rules Football. All had grown up with wealth and privilege, which stood out like dog's balls to someone who hadn't. I watched Lindsay and Hugh surreptitiously. They avoided eye contact or talking directly to each other. A dead giveaway. I wondered if Kate suspected anything.

She looked up and caught me watching her. I looked away. My neck was itchy and I sat on my hands to stop myself scratching. It was already red raw. I was sorry now that I'd come. I was trapped here, in a five star restaurant with a group of pretentious snobs while my daughter ate congealed Pad Thai in a rat-infested warehouse by kerosene lamp. It served her right anyway. She needed to learn that it was her fault she was in this mess. Despite the genes from both parents, it was her choice to embark on a life of crime.

I stood up. 'Excuse me.'

I went out onto the smokers' balcony, took out my mobile phone and called the number of the phone I'd given Frida. She answered straight away.

'Are you okay?' I asked.

'Yeah.'

A group of smokers beside me burst into raucous laughter.

'Where are you?' she asked.

'Having dinner in a restaurant with some friends. Is there anything more you need?'

'A hot shower.'

'Sorry, not included in the budget package.' I sensed a presence behind me. 'Gotta go.'

I pressed the off button and turned around. Kate was behind me. Her silver and black cocktail dress showed off her generous cleavage and hips. Reubenesque was the word. She fumbled in her evening bag, slipped out a cigarette and lit it. She sucked on it as if her life depended on it, then released the smoke as if she were blowing all her problems out into the night air.

'Private phone call?'

'Yes. Not that it's any of your business.'

She raised her eyebrows. 'I couldn't care less. You realise that my husband and your wife are having an affair?'

Of course she knew. If I knew, then she did too. She was no fool.

'Yes. Does he know that you know?'

'Not yet. I thought I'd let him enjoy his birthday and spring it on him tonight. I told him I'll give him his birthday present when we get home. He thinks he's getting a blow job, but I'm giving him the divorce papers all wrapped up with a nice pink bow.'

I was silent, contemplating. Would Hugh fight to save his marriage, or would he and Lindsay use this as an opportunity to come out as a couple? Would I fight to save my marriage? I already knew the answer to that.

'He won't be happy.' There was an unmistakable note of relish in her voice. 'Having to leave the house, all his comforts, spend a fortune on lawyers because I'll take him for every cent he's got and I won't allow him to see the kids. He'll cry and beg me to forgive him and take him back; then when I consider he's grovelled enough, I'll agree to have him back, because I love the selfish, two-timing bastard.'

I stared at Kate. She'd always struck me as an independent woman who could cope with anything. I often wondered what she saw in Hugh. And here she was, planning to do everything she could to make him suffer with the final aim of having him back. Who could make sense of the mysterious workings of women's minds?

She stubbed out her cigarette in the ashtray. 'If I were Lindsay, I'd drop Hugh like a hot potato and get back into your good books. I don't know why she strayed from you, you're a prize catch.' She leaned over and kissed me on the cheek. A soft, lingering kiss. Then flinging her evening bag over her shoulder, she marched back inside.

CHAPTER SIX

Lindsay fixed herself a Tia Maria in a large glass and settled herself on the couch with her iPad. She had a belligerent air about her that often happened when she had too much to drink. Towards the end of the dinner, she'd become embroiled in an argument with Hugh's sister Rachel about the merits of private versus public schooling—Rachel, surprisingly, being an advocate of public schooling. I was about to make her angrier.

I walked over and swiped the iPad out of her hand. 'We need to talk.'

'What are you doing?' She reached for the iPad, but I walked over and threw it onto the kitchen table.

'So you've been fucking Hugh.' Expressions flitted across her face—guilt, fear, anger and finally, the realisation that it would be pointless to deny it.

'So, you're going to tell me that you've been faithful to me over the last 15 years?'

I was silent.

'I thought as much,' Lindsay said. 'But that's not the reason for me and Hugh. You've changed since you became managing director. You used to be so full of energy, such a go-getter. Now it's like the life force has been sucked out of you. You just mope around, you're no fun to be with at all.'

'I'm not the only one who's changed,' I said. 'You used to be bright and funny and sweet. Now you're all bitter and twisted. You drink too much and you spend all your time on Facebook and even though you say you don't, I know you blame me for our not being able to have children.'

'Jesus Christ, don't bring that up again. That's damn well not true.' Her cheeks flushed a dull red. 'And while we're baring our souls, why don't you come right out and admit you never wanted children in the first place?'

'What in hell gave you that idea?'

'I sensed it when we started the IVF. You had this air of detachment about you; sometimes it was like talking to you through a window. You had no idea what I was going through and when I suggested we give it up, it was obvious you were relieved.' Tears were streaming down her face; she made no attempt to wipe them away.

'Just because I didn't talk about it all the time doesn't mean I didn't want children.'

As I said the words, a twinge in my gut made me realise she was more spot on than I cared to admit. It was true I hadn't been sure if I wanted children, afraid that bad parenting was genetic and that I'd be incapable of being a good father after having such a rotten one myself. But I knew how much Lindsay wanted to be a mother and I was prepared to go along with it to make her happy, also knowing that if she fell pregnant, I'd give fatherhood my best shot. The world was full of stories about men who were ambivalent about fatherhood, only to become besotted with their children once they were born.

She was right, too, that she'd needed more support than I could give her. I wanted to reach out and brush the tears from her face. Once, not so long ago, I would have. But now it would feel awkward. And I couldn't be sure she wouldn't slap my hand away.

'I'm sorry things didn't work out the way you wanted,' I said. 'And obviously you'd rather be with lover boy than me, so there's no point in continuing this marriage.'

I went into the bedroom, pulled out a suitcase and threw a few changes of clothes and some toiletries into it. I hauled my sleeping bag and a blanket out of the recesses of the wardrobe, grabbed a pillow off the bed and walked out into the living room.

Lindsay was sitting outside on the patio in the dark with her back to me. I smelt the smoke before I saw the glow of her cigarette. She had given up while she was trying to get pregnant. When did she start again? There was so little I knew about this woman, whom I once knew as well as myself.

I hesitated. Words stuck in my throat. Finally I called out 'Goodbye!' She didn't move, still as a painting, her body silhouetted in the light shining out from the living room. I went into the garage and put my luggage into the boot of the car. I opened the driver's door and was just about to get in, when something caught my eye.

The door of my workshop was ajar, just a tiny crack. I was sure I'd closed it last time I was in there. I walked over, opened it and turned on the light. I surveyed the room; nothing was out of place. The jewellery box was on my workbench in the exact position I'd left it, still handleless. But my sixth sense told me someone had been in here and Lindsay was the obvious person. For what reason? Just being a stickybeak? She would have seen the jewellery box and guessed it was for her. Did she feel a pang of guilt or remorse?

I picked it up and placed it on the cement floor. I fetched a hammer from my tool shelf on the far wall, raised it and with all my strength brought it down on the box, smashing the lid. I pounded until the sweat ran down my neck. Wood flew everywhere, one shard hitting me on the cheek. I dropped the hammer at my feet. The jewellery box was a pile of wood chippings scattered over the floor. Without a backward glance, I turned off the light, closed the door, got into my car and drove away.

#

I parked on the road outside the warehouse rather than driving in, in case the security guy did his rounds and became suspicious of a car parked there in the middle of the night. I grabbed my sleeping bag and pillow, and using the torch on my mobile phone, I trod down the path to the back of the warehouse.

The night was still, a lone owl hooted. The whoosh of traffic on the motorway wafted over on the breeze. With some fumbling, I unlocked the warehouse door. Frida was sitting bolt upright in her sleeping bag, eyes wide with apprehension in the dim glow of the kerosene lamp.

I threw my sleeping bag and pillow on the ground. 'My marriage just broke up, so I thought I'd spend the night here until I decide what I'm going to do.'

Frida looked bewildered. 'It broke up, just like that?'

'It's been coming for a while. I suspected Lindsay was having an affair and tonight I confirmed it.'

'Oh, I'm sorry.' But the words were perfunctory; the same response you give when someone mentions the death of a person close to them whom you didn't know. 'What happened to your face?'

I put my finger up to my cheek, where the wood chip had hit it. It came away stained with blood.

'Did your wife attack you?' Frida asked.

'No, it was just an accident.'

She looked at me as if I'd just given her the male version of the 'I walked into a door' story. In her world, and the world I grew up in, a woman attacking her husband was not an uncommon occurrence.

I went into the toilet, tore off a piece of toilet paper and mopped up the blood. It wasn't a serious cut, it would be healing by morning. I took off my shoes and crawled inside my sleeping bag. Frida watched me as I arranged my pillow and zipped up my sleeping bag.

'Why didn't you have kids?' she asked.

It was a natural question—or was it her intuition at work? I told her the whole story, from the initial medical tests to our decision to quit the IVF.

'We were between a rock and a hard place. If we'd kept on going with no result, it would have ruined our marriage, but deciding to call it quits did the same thing. Even though we both agreed it was the right thing, Lindsay could never come to terms with it. She was an only child and she was desperate for children. And she wouldn't consider adoption.'

Frida gazed into the flame flickering in the lamp. 'I'm not ever having kids.'

'It's not everybody's cup of tea, but you have a lot of years ahead of you to make up your mind for sure.'

'People always say that,' she said fiercely. 'But you shouldn't have kids if you're not 100% sure and I'm not. Not 50%, not even 20%. I don't want to be in the position of stuffing up someone else's life.'

Was she admitting she'd ruined her own life? Strange that we'd both experienced the fear of not measuring up as a parent.

Frida looked sideways at me. 'Did you love Mum?'

Her tone was soft, almost wistful, as if imagining that if I'd loved her mother, we might still be together and she might have had a different childhood. A happier childhood. But I owed it to her to be honest.

'No. But I was young and self-centred. I wouldn't have known what love was if it had bitten me on the arse.'

'So you still would have left, even if you'd known she was pregnant.'

'Yes, I would. I know it sounds selfish, but I had to leave Sydney for my own sanity. It's a small place when you're into crime.' Especially when there's always the chance, however faint, that you could be apprehended for the crime you've never been caught for. That lurks at the bottom of your subconscious like sharks on the ocean floor and wakes you, breathless and sweating, in the middle of the night. 'And having two parents doing drugs would have been no better for you than one.'

Frida was silent for a few moments, then blurted out, 'Danny wanted me to have a baby.'

'Danny?'

'The boy I came down to Melbourne to be with. He introduced me to Teff. He was working for him as a minder.'

'Is that why you broke up? Because he wanted a baby and you didn't?'

'One of the reasons. He was very jealous. He got upset because I had to fuck Teff to get the job, and he started to slap me around. So I packed up and left. No man is going to use me as a punching bag.'

'So that was the criteria for a job with Teff, that you had to sleep with him?'

She gave a wry smile. 'Only the women. But he didn't force me. I did it because it's what I had to do to get the job. Not like Mum. She's so needy and clingy; no wonder men never hang around for long.'

'No serious boyfriend since then?'

'I've had a couple who were serious, but I wasn't.'

Plenty of time for that, you're only young. I stopped myself from saying the words out loud, imagining Frida's reaction to such banal fatherly advice.

'After your scaring the shit out of me tonight, I'm going to go to sleep.' She lay down again and curled up inside her sleeping bag with her back to me. My body was exhausted but my mind was on overdrive. Was I relieved that I left Lindsay? Yes, in the way that making a decision can give you relief. Was I sad? Hell, yeah. The sadness was threatening to overwhelm me, but I pushed it away. Now was not the time to drop my bundle, not when my daughter needed me.

CHAPTER SEVEN

I tossed and turned and it was the early hours of the morning before I drifted off to sleep. I woke at 6.15, my muscles cramped and sore from sleeping on concrete. The morning light was struggling to make it through the window. Frida was still asleep, facing me now, her blonde hair sticking up at all angles, courtesy of Jackson's Shear Horror Salon. Even in sleep, her eyebrows were drawn together in a slight frown. What was she dreaming for about?

There was so much I wanted to ask her. Who did she play with as a little girl? What was her favourite food? What did she want to be when she grew up? What were her dreams now?

She was right, though, I couldn't make up for the missing years in a few days. And in three days, she'd disappear out of my life again.

Her eyes fluttered open. I looked away, but not before I'd seen a flash of little girl shyness; the bashful expression kids get when they realize an adult has been watching them. My heart squeezed. Then the veil came down over her face, shutting me out, as if she thought I'd been divining her inner secrets while she was asleep.

I got out of my sleeping bag and padded up and down the warehouse in my socks to stretch my muscles. Frida yawned and sat up. 'What are you going to do?'

I knew she meant in terms of my marriage. 'I don't know yet. For today, it's business as usual. I'll get you some breakfast, then I'll go into the office. I can shower and dress there.'

'Don't worry about breakfast,' Frida said. 'I've still got some muesli bars and fruit.'

'Will that be enough for the whole day?'

'Plenty. I'm not exactly running marathons in here.'

I nodded at the untouched pile of books. 'Not into romantic comedies?'

Frida rolled her eyes. 'I'd rather sit here and stare at the wall all day.'

I grinned. 'That's one thing we have in common. Sorry, that's all Lindsay reads.' Maybe because her own love life had turned out such a disaster. And there was not a lot of comedy in it.

'Has there been any more in the news about Darcy?' Frida asked.

I took my phone out of my pocket and scrolled through the news sites till I found a report.

'Police are still searching for a slim, dark-haired woman wanted in connection with the murder of health centre owner Darcy Bede earlier in the week. Mr Bede was found in his office shot in the chest. His wife Angelique, a model and popular wellness blogger said, "He was a wonderful husband and father to our two girls. We miss him terribly and we want the f…er who killed him brought to justice."'

'Bullshit,' Frida said. 'He was having it off with half the women in the gym. And she was no better.'

'At least you're no longer dark-haired,' I said. 'And if I keep feeding you, you won't be slim, either.' I slipped my phone back in my pocket and got out my car keys. 'I'll see you tonight. Don't forget to phone me if you need anything.'

'Yes, Father,' she said, with a sardonic emphasis on 'father.' It wasn't the 'Dad,' I'd hoped for, but it would do for now.

#

Celeste gave me one of her subtle once-overs as I walked out of the lift. I'd shaved and showered in the basement bathroom, there for the benefit of those who cycled or ran to work or exercised at lunchtime. Not an enjoyable experience, as the shower ran alternately hot and cold and dwindled to a dribble without warning. My shirt was crumpled from being crammed in my overnight bag and I'd forgotten to pack a tie.

'Lindsay called in a few minutes ago to see you,' she said. Was that sympathy I saw in her eyes?

'Thanks.' I hurried into my office to forestall further conversation.

I cleared my calendar of all non-urgent appointments for the next three days so I could spend as much time with Frida as possible. Over the years, I'd learned that the most important role of a managing director is to delegate, and I'd become so good at it I'd almost done myself out of a job.

My phone pinged with a text message. It was from Lindsay. 'Can we talk some time?'

'It's too late for talking,' I messaged back. I wasn't in the mood for a deep and meaningful discussion, particularly when it was bound to focus on my flaws as a husband.

After an hour answering emails and returning phone calls, I was feeling restless. I didn't want to be in the office in case Lindsay called in again; the sales and marketing office was on the next floor down and it only took her a minute in the lift to get to my office.

I left the office, told Celeste I was going out for lunch, took the lift down to the ground floor, and made my way to the taxi rank on the corner. 'The Crown Casino,' I told the driver.

It was the first time I'd visited The Crown during the day. It was austere in the dull light of the grey clouds, unlike its transformation at night into a gaudy beacon of extravagance and hedonism.

'Good afternoon,' the doorman said cheerily without giving me a second glance. Men in business suits visiting the casino during the day was a common occurrence; but a thrill ran up my spine, as if I were visiting a brothel for a lunchtime liaison.

Entering the gaming area, my pulse quickened as I breathed in the familiar air of anticipation and the desperate optimism that drowned out all sense and reason. I wandered over to the nearest blackjack table and watched the game in action. The players were mainly well-dressed Asians, two of them young women. The man closest to me was on a winning streak, outwardly unmoved as he stockpiled his winning chips. There was a serious intensity in the air I hadn't noticed in the evenings. People were here to win. This was their business, not pleasure.

The back of my neck tingled and not with the usual itch. It was the feeling you get when someone is watching you. I'd been wondering if Jimmy was suspicious of my passport request. Had he put a tail on me? For his own reasons, or on instructions from Teff McGill? Assuming he had links to McGill—but I couldn't assume that he didn't. I'd been on the lookout for someone following me, on foot or by vehicle, but so far had spotted nothing suspicious.

I scanned the table; all eyes were on the nimble fingers of the dealer as he dealt the cards. Ambling over to the cashier, I glanced around me. The surrounding gaming tables were full; no one gave me a second look. Two men in sharp business suits perched on stools at the nearby bar. One met my gaze as I passed then looked away.

A well made-up woman in heels and a tight dress was tottering in my direction. She took me in at a glance the way women do, with an extra dose of hip swagger as she passed me. The eyes of the men at the bar lit up like pinball machines as they watched her approaching the bar. They looked harmless enough, but how could you tell? Suspect everyone and trust no one.

At the cashier's window I paused. I had siphoned money from two joint investment accounts to fund my gambling; one was almost empty, the other still with a few thousand left. So far Lindsay hadn't found out, as she'd had no reason to access the accounts, but it was only a matter of time.

I was balancing on a dangerous threshold. One part of me said, 'Go ahead, your life's fucked anyhow.' The other part said, 'You have a daughter now who depends on you. And you'll need the money to set her up in a new life.'

'Sir? Can I help you?'

The cashier was looking at me, pencilled eyebrows raised.

'Er…no, sorry.'

I stepped aside and the man behind me took my place.

'Hi,' said a soft voice beside me. It was one of the young Asian women from the blackjack table. Petite, glossy black hair, satiny pale skin. She smiled at me, her luscious lips full of promise. 'Would you like a drink?'

The familiar buzz charged my body and hovered around my groin. I knew what was on offer—a drink or two, some superficial conversation and flirtation, then off to one of the hotel rooms in the Casino for hot, no-strings sex. I was working up a sweat just thinking about it, but for once I didn't allow my dick to rule me. I couldn't afford to—for all I knew, this woman could be Jimmy's stooge, part of a setup to lead him or Teff to Frida.

I smiled my regret. 'No thank-you. I'm just about to leave.' And without a backward glance I left.

#

On the motorway from my office to the warehouse there were any number of cars that could have been following me—or just going in the same direction. At the last moment, I swerved over to the left hand lane and onto an exit, then ducked and weaved through the suburban streets until I got hopelessly lost and had to pull over and turn on my GPS. But by that stage I was certain that if anyone had been following me, they'd now be as lost as I was.

The six o'clock news was blaring out of the car radio as I drew up at the warehouse. I was still hyped up from the drive, so I sat for a few moments to calm down. Thank God I hadn't given into the temptation to gamble. Once, it had been a diversion to fill the empty spaces in my life, but at some point the pleasure had become a compulsion. And I hated myself for it. One day I'd tell Frida she'd saved me from making a complete arse of myself.

I got out of the car, with the box of fish and chips I'd bought for dinner, and unlocked the front door. In the drab evening light Frida was on top of her sleeping bag, slouched against the wall, legs sprawled out in front of her, head drooping. The bag of magazines and books I'd brought was beside her, untouched. I shook her gently on the shoulder.

'Wake up, sleepyhead.'

No response. I shook her harder. 'Frida!' Her head lolled down. I put my hand under her chin and yanked it up. Her eyes fluttered half open.

'Frida, what in hell are you playing at?'

She opened her mouth but no sound came out.

'Open your eyes!

She opened her eyes and looked me dully.

'What have you taken?'

She shook her head.

I grabbed her handbag and rummaged around inside it. A wallet, a bundle of tissues, fold-up brush, packet of tampons, two hairclips, tube of lip balm. And a crushed pill packet. Alprazolam. Commonly known as Xanax. The label said Carol Schipp, the date of purchase three months ago.

I opened the packet and slid out three blister cards. All were empty. 'How many did you take?'

She gave a slight shrug.

'Did you take the whole packet just now?'

She didn't respond. I shook her shoulder. 'Answer me, for fuck's sake! Did you take the lot?'

She shook her head. Before I could stop myself, I slapped her face. 'Did you take anything else?'

Her eyes opened wide and she pursed her lips. A globule of spit landed on my cheek.

'Jesus Christ!'

I wiped the spit off on my sleeve. Frida's cheek was bright red. I'd never hit a woman before, though God knows I'd wanted to when I came home from school and found my mother in a pill-induced stupor.

Shame prickled me, but before I could apologise, Frida said slowly, her speech slurred, 'I didn't take anything else.'

'Thank God for that.'

I knew, thanks to my mother, that Xanax, being a sedative, was much more dangerous when taken with other pills or alcohol. The fact that Frida hadn't taken anything else and was conscious and talking suggested that she could recover without medical attention.

I got up and strode over to the grime-streaked window. In my head I ranted and raved. What the hell did you think you were doing? Why would you do such an idiotic thing as steal your mother's pills? Do you realise you'd have jeopardised everything if I had to get medical help?

But there was no point in saying any of those things to her in her present state. When she recovered we'd have a rational conversation, adult to adult, and she'd explain what it was all about and I'd attempt to see things from her point of view.

I sat on the floor and unwrapped the fish and chips. Even the tantalising aroma wasn't enough to make Frida eat. I shovelled them in while she slept, curled up in her sleeping bag. Every now and then, her lips twitched or her eyelids fluttered.

After I'd finished, I moved my sleeping bag closer to Frida's and slid into it. I turned on the kerosene lamp; I didn't intend sleeping. I'd keep an eye on Frida to make sure she continued breathing. It was going to be a long night.

#

I woke with a start. It was still dark, the lamp making a soft puddle of light. I glanced at the luminous face of my watch. 3 a.m. Last time I'd checked it was one 1.45. Despite my best intentions, I'd fallen asleep.

I studied Frida. She was on her side facing away from me, but I could hear her breathing. I had a cramp in my leg and my eyes felt gritty. I slid out of my sleeping bag and padded in my socks up to the end of the warehouse to relieve the cramp and wake myself up.

On my way back, I trod on something. It fluttered and squished under my foot. 'Ugh!' I gasped before I could stop myself. So much for the cockroach baits.

Frida sat bolt upright in her sleeping bag.

'Sorry, I stood on a cockroach.'

She rubbed her eyes. 'What are you doing up at this hour?' Her voice was sleepy, but no longer slurred.

'Looking after you.'

'I don't need looking after.'

'Yes, you fucking do. What on earth got into you, taking those pills? And stealing them from your mother, no less!'

Anger flashed in Frida's eyes and I could see her shrinking into her defensive shell, but I couldn't stop myself.

'Do you realise you would have put us both in danger if I'd had to take you to hospital? With a police alert out for you, someone might have become suspicious, despite your changed appearance. Here I am, jeopardizing my own freedom to help you and you thank me by zonking yourself out on Xanax. Why?'

Frida looked away. When she looked back at me, there were tears in her eyes. 'Because I can't sleep. Every time I close my eyes all I can see is Darcy coming at me with that creepy look on his face and then his body after I shot him. Then when I do go to sleep I have nightmares that he's come back from the dead to try and rape me again. I just wanted to blot it all out for a few hours.'

She scrambled out of her sleeping bag and stood up. 'I'm sorry for the inconvenience I've caused you, and I'm sure that the last thing you wanted right now was for a daughter to turn up and mess up your life. When I get my passport I'll be out of here and you won't hear from me again.'

She marched off and in a few seconds I heard the squeak of the toilet door. So much for the rational, adult to adult conversation. And I, of all people, should have understood what she was going through, with the after-effects of the shooting.

When she returned she crawled back into her sleeping bag and turned her back on me.

'I'm sorry I slapped you,' I said. 'That was unforgivable. My mother was a pill addict and I frequently had to rescue her before she killed herself. It's no excuse, I know.'

Frida was still for a minute. With her back still turned to me, she said, 'Is she still alive?'

'No. She died of a heart attack a couple of years after I moved here. My father died of cirrhosis of the liver six months earlier.'

My throat tightened. I was surprised how much talking about their deaths still affected me after all this time I spent my childhood and adolescence fearing my father's drunken, incoherent rages and despising my mother's withdrawal into the four walls of her bedroom, and after I left home at 15 I had little to do with them.

At their funerals I expected to feel nothing but relief, but I was unprepared for the tidal wave of sadness and regret that swamped me. I never had the time or patience to get to know them, to search below the surface.

Frida had rolled over to face me. I could see she was thinking about the grandparents she'd never known. There was such wistfulness in her eyes that my heart turned over in my chest.

'Do you have any brothers or sisters?'

'I had one brother, Sam, two years older than me. He died of a heroin overdose about 12 months after my mother died.'

I watched her as she took it in. 'So much death,'she said softly.

I nodded, not trusting myself to speak. Her words had loosened the knot inside me that was always there when I thought of Sam. Sam the daredevil, always the first to climb the fence that said 'Trespassers forbidden,' sneak into the cinema without a ticket, break into the school swimming pool for a midnight swim.

And when I plucked up the courage to follow him, he was always the first to take the blame if we got sprung. He was a strange mixture of older brother and father—encouraging me to break the rules, yet enforcing discipline. He never let me wag school and insisted that I do my homework every night, forging my mother's signature to sign it off.

'You're bright, Jackie,' he said. He was the only person I allowed to call me Jackie. 'You should go to Uni.'

But I didn't, I was too busy following in his footsteps. It was Sam who introduced me to drugs and crime; but at some point over the years as he succumbed to heroin's thrall he stopped being my hero, and I became the older brother looking out for him.

'Was it suicide?' Frida asked.

'I don't know. The last time I saw him was six months before he died. He hitched a ride to Melbourne with a friend.'

Just to see me, he said. Which may or may not have been true, but he also hit me up for money. I refused to give it to him, partly because I didn't want him to shoot it up his arm, but also from the lofty perch of self-righteousness of the reformed user.

'He looked pretty bad. He'd been an addict for years; he hated what it did to him but he couldn't stop. He tried a few times, but the white horse always lured him back. When I saw him he had this look about him; that he'd given up, had no will left to fight it.'

What got to me was his acceptance of my refusal to give him money. We were having a drink in my local pub. Sam had a Coke; he hated alcohol. He squeezed my arm and grinned. His hair was limp and greasy, his face a gaunt shadow of itself and he was missing half his teeth, but in his eyes was the spark of the old Sam. The Sam who'd saved me from many a schoolyard flogging by getting beaten up himself, who spent his last cent on football boots for me after our father lost yet another job, who took me to a party and introduced me to hordes of hot chicks after my first girlfriend dumped me.

'It's okay, Jackie,' he said. 'No hard feelings. You'll always be my little brother.' He finished his drink, hugged me and sloped off, shoulders stooped and jeans almost falling off him, the crutch down at his knees.

'I'd like to think it wasn't suicide,' I said. 'It could have just been a batch that was purer than he was used to. But I'll never know for sure.'

It was Sam's funeral that almost derailed me. I went back to Sydney to attend it. I was one of only a handful of people and the only family member; we weren't close to either of our parents' families. Michael McKay, a friend of Sam's from school, turned up and invited me to his house afterwards for 'our own private wake.'

Michael was a member of an outlaw motor bike gang and even though I knew the wake would involve lots of bikies, drugs and gambling, I was sorely tempted. I wanted to fill the emptiness inside me with something and at that moment, I didn't care what. But my instinct for self-preservation kicked in and I refused his invitation. Instead I bought a bottle of bourbon, phoned an old acquaintance and scored some weed and went back to my hotel room. I gorged myself on both until I threw up and drifted into a restless sleep. The next day I felt so ill I rescheduled my return flight to Melbourne to the day after.

'Enough talking about death,' I said. 'We should try to get some sleep.'

A heavy fatigue suffused my entire body—the result of lack of sleep coupled with deep emotion. I slid back down into my sleeping bag.

'I'm wide awake, thanks to you,' Frida said. She rolled over and in two minutes she was emitting tiny snores.

#

It seemed only minutes later that my phone alarm shrilled in my ear. I dragged myself out of my sleeping bag. My entire body ached; sleeping on the hard floor was taking its toll. I staggered down to the toilet.

When I returned Frida was sitting up, sipping from a water bottle.

'How are you feeling?' I asked.

Frida shrugged. 'I've felt better.'

I zipped up my duffel bag and rolled up my sleeping bag. 'I'm not coming tonight. I think I'm being followed and don't want to risk leading them here.'

Frida paled. 'Who's following you?'

'I don't know, I haven't been able to catch them at it, it's just my sixth sense. I think Jimmy may be the instigator; he could be an informant for Teff.'

'But if they're following you they'll know I'm here.'

'I shook them off. You should have seen me zooming up and down the side streets, Mad Max would have been proud of me.'

Far from looking reassured, Frida looked as if she were about to throw up.

'You'll be safe here and if you're feeling scared, I'm only a phone call away.' I checked her food supply; she had enough to last another day. 'As soon as I've picked up your passport tomorrow evening, I'll come straight here and take you to the airport. I'll be on my motor bike; that will put them off the scent.'

I reached over and squeezed her hand. 'Only one more day. We need to make a plan for when we get to the airport.'

'I already have a plan,' Frida said. 'I'll get on the first international flight I can and from there fly to Jamaica.'

'So you're set on Jamaica.'

'It's as good a place as any. And I'd prefer it if you don't hang around after we buy the tickets. I hate goodbyes.'

'So do I. But I'm making sure you get on that plane whether you like it or not. And have you given any thought to how you'll live once you're there?'

'I'll get a job, of course.' Seeing my expression, she added, 'A proper job.'

'So you've landed in a strange country, you don't know anyone, you don't have a work visa, but you're going to walk straight into a job.'

'I'll work it out when I get there. My main concern at the moment is getting out of the country alive.' She blew out a sigh of exasperation. 'I'm twenty-one, not ten. You don't need to do the whole father thing, I can look after myself.'

I exploded. 'It's all right for me to be a father when it comes to doling out thousands of dollars and putting myself at risk helping you to escape the clutches of Teff and the police, but not when I'm giving you some sound fatherly advice. You can't pick and choose, young lady, you get the whole package or nothing.'

I couldn't believe I'd said, 'young lady.' Like every father I ever heard admonishing their teenage daughter. But I didn't care, I'd had a gutful of her prickliness and spoilt child attitude. 'And furthermore, daughters hug their fathers, which is the least you can do after all I've done for you.'

With a resigned expression, Frida got up and put her arms around me. It was tentative, as if it were the first hug she'd ever given, and she wasn't sure how to do it. I wrapped my arms around her and crushed her to my chest, as if I would never let her go.

CHAPTER EIGHT

I showered and dressed in the basement bathroom again and caught the lift to the office. Celeste beckoned me over to the reception desk and nodded towards the open door of my office. A woman was sitting on the couch with her back to me. A very familiar back.

I nodded my thanks for the heads up. Lindsay stood up as I entered. I closed the door. She watched me drop my overnight bag in the corner. It was only two days since I'd last seen her, but the grooves on either side of her mouth were deeper and her usually fresh complexion was an unhealthy grey pallor.

I realised I probably didn't look much better. My head throbbed, my eyes were bloodshot from lack of sleep and an intense itch was spreading over my chest. With a huge effort of will, I refrained from scratching.

'What are you doing here?' I said.

'I want to talk. You won't answer my messages, you're never in the office, you don't come home. I had no other option.'

I had no desire to talk. I figured Lindsay would try to justify her affair with Hugh, and make it sound as if it were all my fault. But if I let her get it off her chest, perhaps she would leave me alone.

I checked my watch. 'I've got a meeting in ten minutes,' I lied. I gestured to her to sit back down on the couch and I took a seat at the other end.

Lindsay angled herself towards me, hands in her lap. 'I just wanted to say I'm sorry.'

'Is that all?'

She nodded. 'I know it's too late, and you think I don't mean it but I do.

You leave a lot to be desired in a husband—you sleep around and run a mile at the slightest hint of uncomfortable emotion, but that was no excuse for me to descend to your level. I should have left you before Hugh and I got together, it would have been more honest.'

That was more like the Lindsay I knew—a virtuoso of the backhanded apology. But it was true that I wasn't up to scratch as a husband. Some men are just not cut out to be married and I'm one of them. But try telling that to a hot-blooded young guy who has fallen for a just-as-hot-blooded woman who makes him feel as if he owns the world.

'Tell me one thing,' I said. 'Why him?'

'Why not him?' She gave me a challenging look. 'Does it hurt your precious ego? Would it have been easier to take if I'd fallen for a Brad Pitt look-alike?'

'I could at least understand it. Hugh is a pompous, shallow twit.'

She shook her head. 'That's where you're wrong. When you take the time to get to know him he's kind and caring and he's not afraid to express emotion. He's really very shy and tries to cover it up; that's why he comes across as arrogant sometimes.'

Proof of the old adage that love is blind. I made a show of looking at my watch and stood up. 'Well, I hope you'll be very happy together.'

She stood up as well. I started forward to open the door for her. She moved in front of me, reached up and ran her fingers across my cheek. My spine tingled. 'I still love you, Jack.'

My throat closed over and I couldn't speak.

'You know what the saddest thing is?' she said softly. 'I don't love Hugh. I'm fond of him but I don't love him in the way that I love you. But you're not going to change, and I don't like the person I am when I'm with you.'

She turned and walked out the door. But not before I saw the glint of wetness in her eyes.

#

I headed home from the office through the grey afternoon drizzle, taking a circuitous route and keeping a close eye on my rear vision mirror. I saw nothing suspicious, but couldn't shake the feeling of being watched.

I drove down the driveway, parked the car in the garage and went into the house, bringing my overnight bag with me. It had been four days since I'd been home; last night I'd slept at a hotel in the city, not wanting to spend the night with Lindsay or alone in the house if she was out with Hugh. It was like a mausoleum in its empty silence. With its five large bedrooms, three bathrooms and expansive indoor and outdoor living areas, it was too big for the two of us. We'd bought it to be a family home; now its lifelessness mocked me.

In the kitchen the only signs of life were a coffee mug and a plate, knife and spoon draining on the dish rack, evidence of Lindsay's usual breakfast of toast and coffee. As I passed through the living room I stopped at the mantelpiece above the electric fire place, where Lindsay had arranged our wedding photos in their gilt-edged frames.

She stood centre stage, swathed in a halo of radiance. Her strapless ivory gown showed off the creamy curve of her shoulders and a tantalising hint of generous cleavage. Somehow she appeared virginal and seductive at the same time. To her left, I stood grinning to cover up my awkwardness at being stuffed into a three piece suit. On her right, Don, tall and craggy-faced, mouth pursed in grim resignation. He and Elaine knew about my past but I hadn't yet proved myself to them. Elaine stood on the other side of me, barely reaching my shoulder. A stout, sweet-faced woman, she took everyone at face value.

She liked me from the start and was the only person who could persuade Don to attend the wedding. Elaine had died two years before Don, also of cancer. It had hit me hard; she was the mother I wished mine had been. One of the last things she said, as I held her withered hand in the hospice was, 'I'm so proud of you, Jack, for your success in the business and making Lindsay happy. I know you'll look after her.'

I turned away and went into the bedroom. After changing into my jeans, weather-proof jacket and boots, I went into my study and opened the middle drawer of my filing cabinet. I retrieved my passport from the P hanger and slipped it into my inside jacket pocket, next to the envelope containing $5000 for Jimmy. Earlier in the day, an idea that had been mushrooming in the back of my mind burst into a moment of clarity and resolve.

Back in the bedroom I hauled two small backpacks from the top shelf of the walk-in wardrobe. Lindsay and I used them for hiking in the early days of our marriage. I transferred my toiletries bag and a change of clothes into one. I'd also taken an extra $19 900 out of the bank—$10 000 per person being the most cash you could take out of the country without declaring it to customs. I divided it into two lots, put the notes into two plastic wallets I'd bought for that purpose and put one in each backpack.

Returning to the kitchen to get a glass of water, I glanced out the French doors of the dining area to the back deck. The right door was ajar; I hadn't noticed it earlier. My head had been so full of other thoughts I also hadn't noticed that the handle and the lock mechanism were hanging out of the door where a large hole had been smashed through it. It looked as if someone had taken a hammer to it. Splinters of wood were strewn over the floor.

I froze, listening intently. Was whoever had broken in still here? Silence. Except for the thudding in my chest. I grabbed an umbrella from the hall stand, the nearest thing to a weapon I could find, and crept through the house, room by room. After an exhaustive search, including the garage and my workshop, I concluded that not only were the intruders no longer there, they'd taken nothing. Which confirmed my theory—that it was Teff's men who had broken in, looking for Frida.

I grabbed the backpacks from the bedroom, went into the garage and stuffed them both into the gear sack bag on the rear of my motor bike. After locking it and slipping the key into my jeans pocket, I wiped the dust off my spare motorbike helmet and hung it on the side hook. I reversed out of the garage, closed the door and roared down the driveway.

#

At 5.45 I was waiting in the public bar of The Pink Elephant in Kew. It buzzed with uber-cool men and women in jeans and ponytails, tattoos peeking out from the sleeves of their business shirts. The men downed boutique beer, the women nursed colourful cocktails. From the tone of the chatter and laughter it was clear that these after-work drinks were the first stop on an end-of-week bender. I felt a stab of envy; I wanted to be young and invincible again, with nothing more serious looming on the horizon than a Saturday morning hangover.

A hand gripped my shoulder and I jumped. Jimmy was grinning at me, impeccable in the same shiny suit. He slid onto the stool beside me and nodded at the soda water I'd bought him.

'Thank you, you are a very considerate man.' I handed him the envelope. He opened it, flicked through the notes, then took out an envelope from his coat pocket and handed it to me.

I opened it up, shook out the passport and looked inside. Laura Jean Hopewell, date of birth 3rd March 1997, the same age as Frida. Born in Adelaide, current address in Doncaster Melbourne, with the photo I'd chosen. The expression on the girl's face was one I'd seen often on Frida's. Stubborn, determined. If Frida could put on that look at the passport control booth, she should pass muster. I flipped through all the pages; it looked as genuine as mine, except for the blank pages.

Jimmy was watching me. 'She will get through customs, no worries. My friend is the best in the business. He asked if you could put a review on Trip Advisor.'

I took a few moments to realise he was joking. I forced a laugh. He laughed too, his eyes crinkling, and clapped me on the shoulder. 'I like you, you understand my sense of humour. That's the problem with this job—you meet so many nice people, then you have to say goodbye.'

He downed his soda water and slipped off his stool. 'Okay, I would love to stay and chat but I have to go. Tell your friend from me, "bon voyage."'

He glided through the crowd and out the door.

\#

The drizzle had stopped, but a misty dampness hung in the air. As I headed through the carpark of The Pink Elephant to my parking spot, I noticed in my peripheral vision a dark-coloured sedan. A man wearing a cap was in the driver's seat. As I glanced around he turned his head, said something to the man in the seat beside him, also wearing a cap, and started the engine. It looked perfectly innocent; two blokes about to drive home from the pub, but an alarm whooped in my head. I had a strong hunch that the driver had started the engine to give that exact impression, to deflect suspicion they were waiting for me.

I slowed right down, dawdling, so they'd have to leave before me. I glanced at the number plate as they drove out and memorised it. They turned left out of the car park, in the opposite direction from the motorway. That at least gave me a head start.

As I merged on to the M1, I looked over my shoulder and spotted a dark sedan about four cars behind me. It was too far away to tell if it was the same one. A Range Rover loomed behind me and blocked my view. It changed lanes; the dark sedan was now three cars behind me. I couldn't see the occupants, but I knew it was them.

I spotted a gap in the traffic, zoomed into the left lane, and down the exit into Glen Iris. I wended my way through the suburbs, checking behind me, but couldn't see any sign of the sedan. I rejoined the M1 at Malvern East. A couple of kilometres along, I spotted it again. Two cars behind me. Fuck— how did they find me again? They were smarter than I'd figured; staying on the M1 on the supposition I'd rejoin it at some point was a safer bet than following me down the exit and losing me.

At the last minute I veered into the exit lane into Chadstone in front of a truck, which gave me a loud horn blast. This time, as I came off the exit ramp to the main road, the sedan was right behind me. I got a closer look at them in my rear view mirror. They both looked young; the driver had a goatee. I zoomed down a side street, then zig-zagged through the suburban streets, past schools, shops and neat brick homes, sometimes doubling back on myself, turning down a side road as soon as I saw a red light.

Being on a motor bike gave me a clear advantage, if I didn't kill myself. I was in Hughesdale before I realised they were no longer behind me; somewhere along the way I had shaken them off. I didn't dare return to the M1, but continued on to Oakleigh via Atkinson Street.

I pulled up at the back entrance of the warehouse, unlocked the gear sack bag, dug out the backpack that was empty apart from the wallet of money and unlocked the door.

Frieda was sitting up in her sleeping bag. The sketch book was on her lap, the packet of pencils on the floor beside her. On the other side lay a pile of empty muesli bar wrappers, an apple core and a half full bottle of spring water.

I threw her the backpack. 'Empty your handbag into this, it's easier to carry. Bring a change of underwear, leave the rest. And hurry.'

She scrambled to her feet. 'What's happened?'

'I was followed after I picked up your passport. I shook them off, but they'll be expecting us to go to the airport, so we need to get there first.'

Frieda stuffed her possessions into the backpack, including the sketch pad and pencils. I turned off the lamp, she followed me out and I padlocked the door.

'Did you see who they were?' she asked.

'Two guys, youngish, wearing caps, that's all I could see. In a sedan, it looked like a Mazda.'

I crammed her backpack into the gear sack bag and handed her the spare crash helmet. 'Have you ridden pillion before?'

She shook her head.

'You'll be fine. Hold on tight and lean in around the corners.'

I got on and started up the engine. Frida climbed on to the rear seat, put her arms around my waist and we took off.

CHAPTER NINE

As we raced along the motorway towards Tullamarine Airport, the city was a blur of lights flashing past us. Deja vu overwhelmed me. I'd done this before, many times. At night Carl and I often brought the girls with us on our joyrides—his girlfriend Amy and Carol. Carl would find a couple of motor bikes parked outside a pub, hot-wire them and the four of us would take off on the motorway out of the city—he and Amy on one, Carol and me on the other.

We didn't care where we went; it was the bliss of riding at night against a backdrop of sky and moon and stars, the wind rushing at our bare faces, our eyes stinging and our lips numb. Carol, her arms tight around my waist, screaming with exhilaration. Listening for the blare of police sirens, knowing that if we got caught, it was worth it for these few minutes. It was a vivid memory that never left me, and it gripped me now. It was not Carol behind me putting her life in my hands, but her daughter. Our daughter. And we were running from someone a lot more dangerous than the police.

I turned off the motorway to the Tullamarine Freeway. An engine roared behind me and lights dazzled my side mirror. I glanced around. A four-wheel-drive truck was almost on my bumper bar, its aggressive headlights blinding me. The driver and passenger both wore caps. Same guys, different vehicle.

I increased the throttle. 'Hang on!' I yelled behind me to Frida as the bike shot up the road. The truck sped up as well. Frida's arms tightened around me and I could feel her terror. I changed lanes, weaving in and out of cars, all the dangerous antics Carl and I had played at and which I now swore at other riders for doing.

I checked my rear-view mirror. Where was the truck? It was behind me again, right on my tail. I swerved into the inside lane before it had the opportunity to run me off the road. My hands were slippery with sweat. All I was aware of was darkness, car headlights flashing past, Frida's arms around my waist and my intense determination not to crash and die.

With relief I saw ahead of me the Terminal Drive exit to the airport and zoomed down it. The truck was two cars behind me. It pulled out into the right-hand lane and came up beside me. I looked up and saw a face sneering at me from the passenger window. The truck veered over the line, coming straight for me. The car in front of me was beetling along at about 80 kilometres an hour. I zoomed around it, a hair's breadth between it and my bike. Frida's arms clenched tighter around my waist; I could hardly breathe.

I stayed in the right hand lane. The truck was two cars behind me, as a car had pulled out into the lane in front of it. At the last minute I veered left into Departure Drive. The truck was right behind me again, like a ferocious monster snapping at my heels. The traffic was slowing down as we came to the drop-off area.

I zipped into a spare parking bay, the truck pulled in behind me. I zoomed out again in between two cars. The truck was blocked by traffic from both directions. I sped down Departure Road, and spotting a service road off to the left, I took it and parked the bike behind an enclave of industrial bins.

I sprang off, Frida behind me. We unstrapped our helmets and I looped them over the handlebars. I pulled our backpacks from the gear sack, threw them both over my shoulder and grabbed Frida's hand. 'Run!'

We raced back on to Departure Drive and headed towards the first entrance into the building. I looked behind me. The truck was just turning into the service road. Fuck. They'd park there and come in after us.

We entered the Departures building and I dragged Frida through the noisy bustle of travellers to the nearest flight departure notice board. She looked over her shoulder. 'Where are they?'

'I don't know, but I doubt they'll try anything in a public place. Keep your eyes straight ahead.'

I searched the departure board. 'There's a flight to London with Virgin at

10.30 tonight.' It was just after 8. 'With luck, there might be a spare seat.'

We hurried over to the Virgin Airlines terminal and stood in the queue for what seemed forever. I didn't dare look around for our pursuers in case it drew attention to me. I took out two caps from my backpack and handed one to Frida. 'Not much of a disguise, but at least it will hide your hair.'

She studied the cap I'd given her. Faded brown, inscribed with 'Bon Jovi. 1993 I'll Sleep When I'm Dead Tour,' above ink silhouettes of the band members. She put it on.

'Hope none of my friends see me wearing this.' She had a sense of humour after all.

I pulled the cap down over her eyes. 'Wear it with pride. Bon Jovi is one of the greatest rock bands ever. I saw them in Sydney on that tour. Unforgettable.' Especially when you were buzzing with eccies.

'Are there any spare seats on the 10.30 to London?' I asked the attendant when we reached the counter.

She tapped on her computer and stared at the screen for a few agonising seconds. 'There's one seat left.'

'I'll book a ticket for my daughter on that flight.' I handed her Frida's passport. 'If I book a seat for myself on the next available flight to London, can I put myself on standby for this flight?'

'We don't provide a standby service,' the attendant replied. 'But if we find there's a seat available prior to boarding, you may have a chance.'

'Thank you. I'd appreciate it if you could do whatever you can. We're going to my mother's funeral. We had very short notice and I won't get there in time if I don't catch this flight.'

Ignoring the waves of anger emanating from Frida, I looked into the attendant's eyes with my most charming smile. She returned my gaze with cool appraisal. 'I'll see what I can do, but no guarantees.'

She tapped away again. 'I'll book you on the flight leaving at 7 a.m. tomorrow morning. May I have your passport please?'

I handed her my passport. Frida dug me in the ribs. 'What are you doing?' she mouthed at me.

I ignored her and focused on the attendant. She opened my passport and scanned it, then opened Frida's. I prayed to the God I didn't believe in that Jimmy's mate hadn't done us over. The attendant looked hard at Frida's photo, then at her, but said nothing. She scanned it and handed them both back.

I breathed an inward sigh of relief and handed Frida her passport; I hadn't had a chance to show it to her. She glanced at it, expressionless, then slipped it into her jacket pocket. I paid cash for the tickets, not wanting to leave a credit card trail. From now on, it was cash only. The attendant handed us our tickets and Frida her boarding pass.

'Do you have any baggage to check in?' she asked Frida.

'Just hand luggage,' I said, pointing to our backpacks.

The attendant raised her eyebrows. 'That's a long way to travel without any luggage.'

'We're going shopping when we get there,' I said.

'Lucky you. If you wait at the departure gate for this flight, the attendants will let you know if there's a seat.'

'What the fuck are you doing?' Frida hissed at me as we headed towards the security check-in.

'I'm coming with you to make sure you get out of the country safely. Think of me as your own personal bodyguard.'

'I don't need a bodyguard. Two of us will be more conspicuous.'

'But two sets of eyes and ears are better than one.'

'How did they make the connection between you and me?'

'I don't know. The only thing I can come up with is Jimmy. Perhaps Teff had forewarned him you'd be wanting a passport, and Jimmy suspected somehow that you were the person I wanted it for.' I remembered my shiver when he laughed and clapped me on the shoulder. 'I wouldn't trust him as far as I could throw him.'

As we approached the end of the security queue, I spied two young punks in jeans, boots and caps, one with a goatee beard, heading through the crowd towards us. Goatee locked eyes with me and pointed two fingers at me, gun-style. A stupid thing to do at an airport, but the gesture was fleeting and no one seemed to notice. Now I knew they were brainless; it made them even more dangerous.

I put my arm around Frida's shoulder, drew her to me and muttered, 'They're over to our right. Don't look; they can't do anything to us here. They'll have to buy a plane ticket to get through security. At least we know they can't get on your flight.'

'Fuck,' she said under her breath. I watched a flustered, middle-aged man take his laptop out of his carry-on bag and empty his pockets on to the plastic tray while his wife barked directions. The couple behind them exchanged sympathetic smiles.

'What will happen to your bike?' Frida said. 'You can't leave it parked where it is.'

'I'll organise something.' There was nothing I could do about it at this moment. I'd taken the keys out, but that wouldn't stop someone stealing it. Or the airport staff impounding it. My only means of freedom in my old life was irrelevant now.

As I placed my backpack, cap and phone on the tray to go through the X-ray machine, I glanced around. The punks had disappeared. Had they gone to buy tickets on another flight so they could get through security and hunt us down? Then they had to find a way to kill us unobtrusively. Still, it wouldn't be wise to underestimate them.

I held my breath as our backpacks passed through the scanner. Even though it wasn't illegal to carry the amount of money we had, it was still a large amount of cash, which might arouse the suspicions of a finicky official. But they passed through without comment. Next was passport control. The officers barely glanced at our passports and as we exited, Frida and I swapped looks of relief.

I steered her past the duty free store, bars and souvenir shops to a clothing store called Mulberry. The mannequins were dressed in jeans, colourful tunics and sweaters and jaunty berets.

"We're going on our shopping spree now,' I said. 'If we're wearing different clothes it will help put those thugs off the scent. And don't forget your name is Laura.'

The young assistant was getting ready to close the shop, but I persuaded her to stay open a bit longer, intimating I'd be making a few purchases. As it was winter in London, I bought myself a pair of black jeans, a striped jumper and a mulberry coloured overcoat. Not the sort of gear I would normally have chosen, but what the hell. Now was as good a time as any to update my style.

Frida took me at my word when I told her to buy what she wanted. She chose a pair of jeans fashionably ripped at the knees, a tunic top, a long sleeved jersey and a fake-fur lined jacket. I stopped myself from telling her that 'normal' jeans would be warmer; at her age being cool was worth the discomfort of knees like blocks of ice. The assistant beamed as I handed her a wad of cash, happy that her decision to stay open had been vindicated.

We went into the nearest restrooms to swap the clothes we were wearing for our new gear. I made sure there were others in the male restroom before I went in, in case the punks were hovering around and had any ideas about popping me off while I was in there.

I was first out, and as I waited for Frida, I sent two text messages. One to Celeste to tell her I was going away and to reschedule all my appointments for the next week, and the other to Lindsay. 'DO NOT GO HOME. The house has been broken into and your life is in danger. Find somewhere to stay for a few days. I'll be in touch soon.'

I imagined the reaction that message would get. As I pressed the 'send' button, a message came through from a number I didn't recognise. I clicked on to it.

'Hi Jack, it's Carol. I'm using a friend's phone. I've been trying to contact Frida but she won't answer her phone. A couple of thugs came round wanting to know where she was. They beat me up pretty bad, but I didn't tell them. They stole my phone and I'd put you in my contacts, so I guess they'll find you. Sorry I didn't tell you sooner, I just got out of intensive care. Lucky I remembered your number—the old brain still works sometimes! Please answer as soon as you get this.'

When Frida reappeared from the Ladies in her new clothes, I passed the phone to her. 'Here's our answer about how those goons found us.'

As she read the message, her eyes brimmed with tears. 'Those fucking bastards. I wish I still had that gun. I'd hunt them down and kill them.'

'Your mum's tough, she'll survive it.' Carol's need for approval left her vulnerable to abuse, but on this occasion she'd suffered life-threatening injuries for the sake of her daughter's safety. I felt a new respect for her and wondered if Frida was the one thing that had kept her alive all these years.

I sent a message back. 'Frida is okay. Can't say any more. Will be in touch later.'

I checked my watch. 'They'll be calling your flight any minute. If I can't get on your flight, here's the plan. There's nine thousand dollars in your backpack. As soon as you get to Heathrow, change five hundred into pounds at the foreign exchange and get a room in a hotel close to the airport. Wait there and don't go anywhere, don't leave your room. Order room service for your meals. I'll text you when I arrive, you can take a cab to the airport and we'll buy our tickets to Kingston.'

'Our tickets?' Frida said.

'What sort of a bodyguard would I be if I didn't accompany you all the way? I hear Jamaica is very nice at this time of year.'

#

As we made our way to the departure gate for Frida's flight, a voice boomed over the loudspeaker. 'Would Mr Jackson Forbes please go to gate 44. Mr Jackson Forbes to gate 44 please.'

'So much for keeping a low profile,' I muttered.

At gate 44 the attendant said, 'Mr Forbes? We've managed to get you a seat on this flight. Can I have your passport and ticket please?'

While he scanned them and tapped away on his computer, I looked around. No sign of the punks. 'Can't see them,' I murmured to Frida. 'Doesn't mean they're not here.' Another announcement over the loudspeaker called for passengers on the flight to London to proceed to gate 44. Those sitting in the departure area collected their belongings and queued up.

The passengers at the head of the queue had already trooped through the exit to the plane when the attendant handed me back my passport with my new ticket and boarding pass.

'I'm sorry, I wasn't able to get you a seat next to Ms Hopewell,' he said.

'No worries,' I said. I turned around and looked straight into the eyes of

Goatee. Standing two metres in front of me, hands in his pockets, grinning. An idiotic schoolboy grin, as if he'd spied me smoking behind the toilets. His mate, shorter and dark-haired with a Mediterranean look about him, glowered at me.

Frida gasped. I thought she was about to run, but there was nowhere to go. I walked up to Goatee and got up right into his face, so I could see the bristles where he hadn't shaved and smell the cigarette smoke clinging to his clothes. 'Tell McGill I'm insulted that he's sent a couple of goons after us. We deserve better than that.'

Goatee's grin wavered. His eyes darkened.

'Better still, tell him to lay off completely. He won't win this one.'

Goatee's grin widened again. His mate opened his mouth as if to say something but Goatee put his hand up to stop him. 'Bon voyage,' he said. He pointed his two-finger gun at me, then they both turned and sauntered off.

'Fuck,' breathed Frida, watching them. 'What did you say to them?'

'Just told them to tell Teff to leave us alone.'

'As if that will make any difference.'

'It won't, it just made me feel better. They're a couple of idiots. When they couldn't run us off the road, they knew they were beaten.' The unspoken certainty hung in the air between us; Teff would have bigger plans up his sleeve.

'Now they know we're going to London,' Frida said as we joined the end of the queue.

'We'll be out of there before they can catch us,' I replied, with more conviction than I felt.

#

In the end, Frida and I were able to sit together, due to the obliging passenger next to me who swapped seats. The eight hour journey to our stopover at Dubai seemed like an eternity. Frida put on her headphones as soon as the plane took off and watched a movie. I tried to do the same, but couldn't concentrate.

I finally drifted off and found myself in the middle of an armed robbery in a store with Frida as my accomplice. Teff was behind the counter. He pulled his gun and aimed it at me, then pointed it at Frida and shot her in the chest. She slumped into me and I tried to catch her as she fell to the ground. My devastation that I'd failed to protect her was so intense I thought I'd die myself.

I awoke, breathless. The same nightmare I'd been having for twenty odd years; just a different cast of characters. Frida was asleep with her head on my shoulder. She still had that slight frown, her face had a clammy sheen to it and she was restless and twitchy. I wondered if she was having nightmares as well. When the flight attendant came by with the drinks trolley, Frida opened her eyes and looked blearily around. I waved the flight attendant away and Frida dropped her head on my shoulder again and went back to sleep. I didn't move for the rest of the journey.

We staggered off the plane at the Dubai International Airport at 6.30 a.m. I felt like a chewed up rag and Frida didn't look much better. We found a table at a cafe and I bought us coffees.

'Luckily we didn't need Plan A,' I said. 'Here's Plan B. When we arrive we book the first flight available to Kingston. If we have to stay overnight we'll book into a hotel near the airport.'

'How long are you staying in Jamaica?' Frida asked.

'Long enough to see you settled.'

I didn't want to make her more afraid by telling her the real reason—that I didn't trust Teff not to track her down, even in Jamaica. If we made it there. Airlines weren't permitted to release information about passengers and their destinations, but you could always get round those rules if you knew the right people.

When Frida went to the Ladies I turned on my phone. I'd had several missed calls from Lindsay after my text message, then obviously fed up with not getting an answer, she'd replied by text. 'What do you mean, my life is in danger? What the hell are you playing at? Did you call the police about the break-in? Please answer me, Jack.'

Then another message, sent two hours later. 'Where's the money from the investment accounts? Let me guess—you threw it all away at the Casino. And of course you conveniently disappeared to avoid facing up to it. You gutless prick. I'll take you for everything you've got. Where are you???'

She was right; I was a gutless prick. As for taking me for everything I had, she was welcome to it, though it wouldn't begin to make up for all my sins. But I owed her a personal explanation. Of sorts.

I phoned her and she answered it on the second ring. 'Jack, what the hell is going on?'

'I can't tell you; it's best for your own safety that you not know. I'll be away for a few weeks. I'm really sorry about the money, Lindsay.'

'I won't care about the money if I'm dead. You can't tell me my life is in danger and then not tell me why. What have you got yourself into, Jack?'

'I had to do something for someone that meant some involvement with people on the wrong side of the law. That's all I can say and I'm very sorry you've been dragged into it. The best advice I can give you is not to go back to the house. Sell it if you want; you wanted to move anyway.'

'I wanted to move in my own time, not because some criminal has got it in for me because my soon-to-be ex-husband has pissed him off. I can't believe you've done this after all these years of being straight. Why?'

I was silent, trying to think of a way to explain it without bringing Frida into it.

'Of course, you can't tell me for my own safety. Is that why you took the investment money?'

'No, that had nothing to do with it.' At least that was one truth I could tell her. 'I gambled that away because I was unhappy. A stupid thing to do, I know.'

Lindsay blew out an angry sigh. 'Stupid doesn't even begin to describe it. I've been unhappy too, you know.'

'I know.'

I spied Frida coming towards me. 'Lindsay, I've got to go. I'm getting rid of this phone shortly so don't try ringing me. I'll be in touch again when I get to my destination. I'm sorry for…'

The phone beeped in my ear. Lindsay had already ended the call.

#

Back on the plane I made note of the new passengers in the vicinity of our seats. A dark-skinned man in a business suit with a briefcase; a tiny, striking Asian woman in jeans and high heels; and a solidly built guy with a shaved head and tattooed neck. Did Teff's power and influence extend outside his own country? Was Goatee's two-finger gun just an attempt to scare us, or was it a serious threat? Even if Teff had contacts in Dubai, it seemed unlikely that they'd buy a ticket on this flight, follow us when we arrived in London and bump us off. The tattooed guy looked like a typical gangster, but he was probably a hairdresser who liked cats and yoga.

It was much more likely that Teff would have someone waiting for us at Heathrow, hiding in the crowd and discreetly following us until they got a chance to kill us. What were the chances of my being able to spot them? Finding a hitman at an international airport was like trying to find a flea on an old English sheepdog.

Time didn't just crawl; it dragged itself along with a limp. I managed a restless nap and Frida watched more movies. I woke up with Frida dozing on my shoulder again. The sketch pad was on her lap. It was open, revealing a rough pencil sketch.

It was the back view of a man sitting in a seat. Studying the drawing, I realised it was the man across the aisle, in the row ahead of her. She'd captured his balding head with its few wisps of hair, his neck retreating into his jacket and the broadness of his shoulders. She'd used just a few pencil strokes blended with adroit shading to achieve these effects.

I slowly reached out to lift the page to see if she'd done any others. The moment I moved, her head bobbed up and her eyes sprang open. Noticing my gaze, she slapped the sketch pad shut.

'I thought you said you weren't any good at art,' I said.

'I'm not.'

'It looks pretty good to me.'

'Your opinion is hardly objective, though.'

'Doesn't mean it's not valid.'

She didn't reply. I thought of the years I'd missed, of her bringing works of art home from school. Of my telling her how great they were and sticking them on the wall. She'd have lapped up my praise then. The flight attendant materialised with another meal and Frida stuffed the sketch pad and pencils back into her backpack.

We landed at Heathrow mid-afternoon and stood in the interminable queue at immigration. When it was our turn, the official examined our passports.

'From Aussie land, I see.'

'Yes,' I said.

He looked up, studying us both.

'Business or pleasure?'

'Pleasure,' I said. His gaze didn't waver as he waited for me to expound upon it. People who had something to hide often talked to cover up their nervousness; I wouldn't make that mistake.

'What sort of pleasure?' he said. His words had an undertone of belligerence I've often noticed in men who get a kick out of asserting their authority.

'Sightseeing,' I said. Then, realising that saying too little could be just as suspect as saying too much, I added,' My daughter's never been to London before, so I'm showing her around.'

'Is that so? Well, there's plenty to see.' He thumbed through the blank pages in Frida's passport. 'So it's your first time overseas, Laura?'

'Yes.'

'We'd better give you a stamp then.'

He stamped both our passports and scanned them. 'I've heard that you Aussies have kangaroos to help you with your shopping.'

Now it was our turn to stare at him.

'You put all your groceries in their pouch, instead of a supermarket trolley.'

'That's true,' I said. 'I keep a couple in my back yard for that very purpose.'

He gave a grin that didn't reach his eyes. He handed us back our passports.

'Have a lovely time, folks.'

He made 'a lovely time' sound as if it were something underhanded. Or maybe it was just my being paranoid.

As we walked away, a voice behind me called out, 'Excuse me, sir!'

I turned around. The official was beckoning us back. Shit. Stay calm. It will probably be another kangaroo joke.

'I know Aussies love their fish and chips. You should go to Toffs, best fish and chips in London. In Muswell Hill.'

'Thanks for the tip,' I said. He waved me off as if to say, 'It's nothing.'

'Business or pleasure?' I heard him say to the next in line.

'What a dickhead,' Frida said.

'That's for sure. So far so good. We're halfway there.'

Frida looked around at the swirling tide of humanity, hurrying, chattering, laughing. A nearby child let out a travel-tired wail, drowning out all the surrounding noise.

'Take it all in,' I said. 'This might be all you ever see of London.'

As we headed for the arrival lounge, I spotted the tattooed guy and the young Asian woman waiting in the crowd around the luggage carousel. The dark-skinned businessman already had his suitcase and was embracing a young woman in a headscarf, three young chocolate-skinned children dancing around them. I bought us takeaway coffees and searched on my phone for the next flight to Kingston. British Airways, tomorrow at 8 a.m.

'You're in luck, there are two seats available on that flight.' The attendant at the British Airways reservation counter printed out our tickets and handed them to us. The caffeine had kicked in and I was alert for anything or anyone out of the ordinary as we made our way to the hotel reservation desk. Quicker and easier than booking it online. All I wanted to do was stand under a hot shower and sink into a real bed.

We joined the end of the queue. The young Asian woman was at the front. 'Thank you very much,' she said. As she moved off, I caught her eye. She arched her eyebrow just a fraction and her generously-enhanced lips turned up. My stomach jolted. Was that just an ordinary flirtation or was there something more sinister behind it? Surely she wouldn't be so obvious, but maybe that was part of the bluff.

I glanced at Frida, standing beside me. She was looking pointedly away, like every kid who hates being witness to their parent's interest in the opposite sex.

When we reached the counter, the attendant booked us a room at the Blue Ibis, a 4 star hotel two kilometres from the airport. Her computer froze just as she was completing the booking, so she had to phone the hotel. As the receptionist kept her on hold, she smiled an apology to the man behind me.

'It's all right, love, I'm not in a hurry,' the man said. He sounded like one of the Beatles, a Liverpudlian perhaps. Of all the nationalities mingling here, it was strange to hear a native. Our booking completed, we headed to the exit.

As we waited at the taxi rank in the afternoon gloom, the wind whipped the bare trees and the cold seeped in through my new sweater and coat. Frida huddled into her jacket. One more night and we'd be in Jamaica, where the temperature rarely dipped below 25°C, even in winter, if my brief internet research was correct.

In my mind's eye I saw the shimmer of aqua ocean, palm-dotted beaches and verdant tropical gardens, and for a few moments I entertained the fantasy that we were doing nothing more perilous than going on a much-needed holiday.

In the cab, something was needling me about the queue at the hotel reservation desk. Was it the Asian woman? Or was that just my dick talking? No, it wasn't her, but if I stopped thinking about it, maybe it would come to me. I kept an eye on the rear window of the cab; there was a steady stream of traffic going in the same direction. Impossible to tell if anyone was tailing us.

At the Blue Ibis we checked in and put the clothes we weren't wearing into the express laundry service, so we'd have fresh clothes for the next day. In the lift to our room on the tenth floor, Frida said, 'Was someone following our taxi?'

'Not that I could see. But to be on the safe side, we need to stay around other people when we're not in our room, and if anyone knocks on the door, don't answer it.'

Our room, with one queen bed and one single, was basic but comfortable. It was while I was in the shower that I remembered. The Liverpudlian man behind me at the hotel reservation desk had been listening to my conversation with the attendant as she was booking our room. As I replayed the scene in my mind it struck me that it wasn't just the idle act of someone waiting their turn; he was listening as if he wanted to know the details of our accommodation.

I'd glanced around at him when he joined the queue. Medium height, stocky build, early thirties, buzz cut. Nothing remarkable about him, but I was sure I'd recognise him if I saw him again.

After Frida showered and dressed we went down to the restaurant for dinner. I looked around as the maitre d' led us to a table but couldn't see Mr Liverpool. Not that I expected to; if he were a hired killer he'd be keeping a low profile. Especially since he knew I'd seen him.

After we ordered our drinks, Frida said,' When you go home, Teff will find you and make you tell him where I am.'

That had occurred to me, but I wasn't going to let Teff McGill run my life. Which was easy to think when I was out of the country.

'You concentrate on your new life as Laura Hopewell and let me deal with Teff.'

'So you'd let them kill you rather than tell them my whereabouts?'

'If that's what it takes.' The certainty was there, in the pit of my stomach. That's what you do for your child.

She was silent, but her disbelief was plain. When did youth come to be synonymous with cynicism? 'You think you're so grown up,' I wanted to say, ' but you're just a babe in the woods.'

The waiter appeared to take our order. Frida ordered the most expensive dish on the menu, baked lobster stuffed with shrimp. I ordered the Steak Diane with salad. Lindsay always teased me about my simple tastes in food, but I guess that was my working class origins coming to the fore.

'I wish I had time to show you around London,' I said. 'It's so full of tradition and history.'

'When were you here?'

'On my honeymoon. It was part of a trip around Europe.'

The differences in our temperament had become unavoidably apparent. Lindsay wanted to cram in as much as possible, as if afraid of missing something vitally important. I was keen to see the sights, but I also wanted downtime to lounge in the cosy pubs enjoying a beer, or on the bank of the Thames, scoffing some of the legendary English fish and chips.

After four days of non-stop sightseeing, I rebelled. Lindsay wanted to go to some obscure museum. 'You go,' I said. 'I'm going to sit in the pub down the road and chill out." She went off in a huff and came back three hours later to find me half shot and laughing uproariously with a group of backpackers. She became even more furious and refused to talk to me for the rest of the day—until later that night when I managed to entice her over to my side of the bed.

Consequently, we both arrived back from our honeymoon exhausted instead of refreshed.

'Do you think your wife would have married you if she'd known about me?' Frida asked.

'Hard to say. But I may not have met her at all if I'd known about you. My life would have been completely different. And who knows, I might have been able to prevent you from getting into the trouble you're in now.'

'So do as you say, not as you do?'

'You might have learned something from my mistakes.'

'You think your influence would have had that much effect on me?'

She gave me one of her surly looks. I couldn't help grinning. 'I guess not, you're as stubborn as a mule. I don't know where you got that from.'

After dinner I went to the bar and chose two bottles of wine to take up to the room.

'We'll have room service deliver them to you,' the barman said.

'I'll take them up myself, thanks.'

As he handed me the bottles, the barman gave Frida, standing beside me, the once over. I knew what he was thinking. He can't wait 20 minutes for the wine to be delivered, he wants to get her drunk and quickly. And she's young enough to be his daughter.

'I'll explain upstairs,' I said to Frida, as we headed to the elevator.

Back in the hotel room I told her about my suspicions of Mr Liverpool.

'Him?' she said. 'He was standing pretty close; I thought he was trying to get a look at my tits.'

'He may well have been, but I have a bad feeling about him. If he's a professional killer, he'll have no problems finding out which room we're in and breaking in.'

I pointed to the bottles of wine I'd placed on the shelf next to the coffee percolator. 'I have a plan. And those bottles are part of it.'

I told her my plan. "Do you think you can do it?"

She nodded.

'Part A, coffee.'

I fired up the percolator and made us both a cup of strong coffee. We would need it to stay awake all night.

#

I found a movie on the TV and we settled in the two armchairs. It was a B-grade crime movie with no actors I recognised and the usual shootings and car chases. I was watching it, but not seeing it and when I glanced at Frida I could see her mind was far away as well. Her face was taut and she was biting her lip.

I picked up the remote control and muted the sound. 'Are you scared?'

For a moment I thought she'd deny it, then she nodded. Her eyes filled with tears and she brushed them away.

'Me too,' I said. 'Are you thinking about Darcy?'

She nodded. 'I can't stop it. Even when I'm not thinking about him, it's in my mind. That look on his face before he attacked me...I can't believe I killed a man. I mean, he was an arsehole, but. ... 'Her voice trailed away.

'If it's any consolation, I know what you're going through. I've killed a man, too.'

She said nothing, as still as a statue. It seemed as if the whole world had shrunk down to the four walls of this room. Holding its breath. Waiting.

I got up, paced to the opposite wall and back again. 'My mate Carl Mooney and I were doing over a liquor store. It was late at night, the only place open in a small suburban shopping centre, one old guy. Near closing time, so we knew he'd have a lot of cash. I waved a gun at the guy and told him to empty the till, but he reached down behind the counter and pulled out his own gun. I shot him in the chest. He died instantly.'

I was inside the nightmare again. All the details I hadn't registered at the time—the old guy's mottled bald head shining under the fluorescent light,

Carl's rapid, shallow breathing beside me, the chemical odour of the plastic mask on my face—were magnified a hundredfold. Then I realised it wasn't Carl's breathing I was hearing, it was mine.

'I was in shock for a few seconds, then I grabbed Carl by the arm and said, "Let's go."

'He said, "What about the money?"'

'"Forget the money,' I said, "we're in deep shit."'

'We raced outside, ducked down a few side streets, took off our masks and threw them into an industrial bin. Then we went into the nearest hotel and had a drink to give ourselves an alibi, hoping that if it came to the crunch, we'd say we'd been at the pub for half an hour before the robbery and no one else there would remember the exact time we came in.'

My feet were firm on the floor and my hands clenched, but my entire insides were trembling. I hadn't told a single soul about this—not Lindsay, because I wasn't sure how much 'bad boy' she could handle. Not Carol, not even Sam, who'd become a stranger, emaciated and dead-eyed. I was too afraid that one of them would blab to save their own skin next time they had a run-in with the cops.

'We were never caught, never even questioned. I read about it in the newspapers. I didn't want to know anything about the man I shot, but I couldn't help it. His name was Arthur O'Keefe. He was 75, going to retire in a few months. He owned the bottle shop with his son. He had three kids, eight grandchildren, played lawn bowls, went to the club with his mates; a normal, everyday guy.'

'Carl kept saying, "Don't worry, he was an old man. He would have kicked the bucket soon anyway. It's his own fault—if a man points a gun at you, of course you're gonna shoot him, it's either you or him."'

'But I knew it wasn't right. I believe there are two things that happen after you kill someone for the first time—you vow you will never do it again, or you justify it to yourself and continue down the path where you'll likely end up killing again. Most of the guys I hung out with were in the latter category and I didn't want to be one of them any longer. That's when I decided to get out of that life. What's the saying? Reinvent myself.'

I looked her in the eye. 'I was only three years older than you are now.'

'I get the point.'

'There is no point. I'm just telling you my story.'

'What happened to Carl?'

'He was killed in a siege shootout a couple of years later. By a cop.'

It could have been me. The unspoken words hung in the air.

'Do you still feel guilty?' Frida asked.

'Hell, yes. Never a day goes by that I don't think about it. I still have nightmares.'

'Have you ever thought about giving yourself up?'

'Lots of times. But the upshot is that Arthur is dead and nothing can change that. I decided that by going straight I was paying my debt to society, although I know the courts wouldn't see it that way. But there's one overriding factor why I haven't.'

'You don't want to go to jail?'

'You got it. Call me selfish, or a coward, I'll wear it. Sometimes I tell myself that dragging the guilt and memories around with me is a worse punishment than jail, but that's bullshit. Nothing could be worse than losing my freedom.'

Or the illusion of freedom.

'We're stuck with each other now,' Frida said. 'We both know each other's dirty secrets.'

It wasn't the most desirable basis for a father-daughter relationship. But it was a start.

Frida nodded to the two bottles of wine I'd bought. 'Can we open one and have a glass?'

'Absolutely not. We have to keep our wits about us.'

#

At 10.30 p.m. I gathered some cushions from the chairs and towels from the bathroom, rolled them up and placed them under the covers of the queen bed, arranging them to look like a person huddled under the covers.

It was woeful. It looked exactly what it was—a bunch of towels and cushions under the covers. Frida grimaced in mock exasperation, pulled out the towels and cushions and re-arranged them. When she'd finished, I could have sworn there was someone in the bed. She collected more cushions and towels and did the same with the single bed.

'You do have artistic talent after all,' I said.

'Don't think there's much call for that sort of talent. What would you call it—bed sculpting?'

'Whatever it's called, it's come in very handy.'

At 11 p.m. I turned off the TV and all the lights and closed the curtains. We went into the bathroom, to the immediate right of the front door. I brought in both bottles of wine, opened them and tipped the contents down the sink. 'Lambrusco,' I said. 'Only good for cleaning drains.'

I turned off the bathroom light and we set ourselves up for the night behind the open bathroom door, both armed with an empty wine bottle, Frida sitting on the lid of the toilet and me standing.

I listened to the muffled sounds of the TV from the room next door. After half an hour, they stopped and we waited in silent darkness. I'd felt an instant release after divulging my secret to Frida; speaking the words out loud had lifted the burden that had been there so long it had become a part of me, like carrying a few kilos of extra weight. But it was only temporary; I would never be rid of the guilt.

I forced my thoughts back to the present; I needed to be alert for the slightest sound. If this was all for nothing, I'd have no trouble sleeping on the plane tomorrow.

Once my eyes were accustomed to the darkness, I checked every now and then to make sure Frida hadn't nodded off to sleep. Each time she gave me a thumbs up. Once I squeezed her hand. It was as cold as doom.

Just when I was thinking this was a stupid idea and my imagination had got the better of me, I heard a tiny noise. A light scraping sound in the front door lock. I sensed rather than heard the door open. I signalled to Frida; she was already on her feet.

The door closed with a faint click. Footsteps crept in. I held the bottle up in front of me, ready for him if he looked in the bathroom. He didn't. I moved into the doorway of the bathroom and made out a figure approaching the single bed.

I crept up behind him and raised the bottle. He spun around, a gun in his hand, the silencer pointed at me. I crashed the bottle over his head. The bullet flew past me and hit the wall. Thwack.

The man pitched forward on to the floor. I threw myself on top of him, feeling in his hand for the gun. It wasn't there. I rolled off him, groping around on the floor. He threw himself on top of me and punched me in the back of the head. Light flashed before my eyes and my head spun. I elbowed him in the groin and he released his hold enough for me to turn over and land a punch on his jaw.

He tackled me to the floor, then had his hands around my neck. His body odour was strong, his grip powerful. I couldn't breathe, I was choking. Where the hell was Frida? Then she was above us, wine bottle poised. As she brought it down, the man moved his head and she clipped him on the ear.

He flopped forward, and I rolled out from under him, coughing and gasping. I groped around behind the bedhead for the gun. I felt its cold metal and inched it closer. The man sprang on top of me again, reaching over me to grab the gun. Frida jumped on him, the bottle in her hand. He reared up, smacked her in the face and sent her sprawling.

The diversion was just enough time for me to reach out and take hold of the gun. As the man lunged at me, I aimed the gun and put a bullet in his head.

CHAPTER TEN

The man flopped forward and sprawled across me. I pushed him off and sat up. 'Frida, are you okay?'

'Yes.' It was a whimper. I felt for the bedside lamp and turned it on. Frida was lying on the floor. Blood trickled out of her mouth, her cheek was red and swollen and her right eye was beginning to turn black. She looked at me, got to her feet and dashed into the bathroom, coughing and retching.

Wetness was soaking into my shirt. I looked down; it was spattered with blood and brains. I grabbed a towel from under the covers of the bed and wiped myself as best I could. My head was pounding from the punch. I rolled the man over onto his back. Impossible to tell what he'd looked like with half his head blown off, but he had a similar height and build to Mr Liverpool.

Frida emerged from the bathroom, averting her gaze from the body. I put my arms around her; she shivered and shook like a frightened bird.

'You came in not a moment too soon. That bastard's hands had the strength of ten men. I couldn't hold out much longer against them.'

I touched her cheek. 'I'm sorry you had to get hurt in the process.'

'You should see yourself. And you wouldn't have been here at all if you weren't saving my life.'

I grinned. 'Well, there is that.'

She smiled. A smile made even more beautiful by her swollen cheek and black eye, against the backdrop of a dead body, carpet glinting with shards of glass and a wall splattered with blood and brains.

#

'We have to get rid of the body,' I said. I racked my brains; places to hide a body in the middle of the night without being seen were hard to come by in hotels.

'I'll be back in a sec.' I opened the door and went out into the brightly-lit, carpeted corridor. I passed half a dozen rooms before coming to an alcove with a drink machine. I'd remembered seeing someone getting a drink from it as we were coming out of our room to go to dinner. There was enough room between the side of the machine and the alcove wall to stuff a body. It would be visible to anyone walking past and it wouldn't take long for someone to raise the alarm, but at least there'd be nothing to link it to us. We were checking out early, and I could only hope that by the time the police arrived and started their investigations, we'd be on our flight.

Frida helped me drag Mr Liverpool out of the room and down the corridor. We averted our eyes from the mess which once was his head. Frida looked as if she might be sick again, but she held herself together. We hauled the body into the space beside the machine and left him lying there on his side with his legs drawn up to his chest, so they didn't protrude out into the corridor.

Back in the room I wiped the gun, wrapped it in a plastic bag and placed it in my backpack. I'd dispose of it in an industrial bin before we went to the airport. We picked up all the broken glass from the carpet and put it in the rubbish bin. I washed the towel I'd used to wipe myself down and hung it up to dry, wiped the blood and brain matter off the wall with toilet paper and flushed it down the toilet.

By now it was 2.30 a.m. Sleep was out of the question. We showered and changed into the clean clothes the hotel had delivered while we were at dinner. My head was still throbbing; I hoped there was no permanent damage. I made us both another cup of coffee and we drank it sitting on my bed.

'You broke your promise to yourself,' Frida said.

'Yeah.'

I'd vowed never to kill again, I'd have staked my life on it. Fate laughs at you when you make a promise like that. You're so sure you know yourself, but you don't.

'I guess I didn't anticipate having to shoot someone to save my life.'

'It was me he was after.'

'He would have killed us both.'

Did Mr Liverpool have a wife, kids, siblings? Someone somewhere would mourn him. Someone who loved him, would feel the numbness of shock and the ache of grief, the enormity of the gap he left in their world, would rail at the randomness and unfairness of his death. I had to stop thinking like this, it was the way to madness. He was a professional killer, the risk of being knocked off came with the territory. And while killing someone to save your own life is understandable, doing it to save someone else's life is surely a more heroic act. Funny, but I didn't feel like a hero.

I glanced at Frida. Her eye was now sporting tinges of purple. 'You okay?' I said.

She nodded.

'Better put your cap and sunglasses on when we check out. I don't want people thinking I did that.'

I got up and drew the curtains back and we watched the dawn seeping through. Another day, a new beginning. How long had it been since I watched the sun rise and felt the stirrings of hope?

'What do you want to do with the rest of your life?' I said.

'You sound like the counsellor they made me go to at school. I said leave home and make lots of money.'

'Which you did,' I said. 'Now you need some new goals.'

She stared out the window. A jet streaked through the sky in the direction of the airport, trailing a plume of smoke. The early morning arrivals had begun. I thought of the passengers, tired and bleary-eyed, eager to touch solid ground and begin their holiday, reunite with loved ones, or return home. Wherever you were, you always wanted to be somewhere else.

'When I was a kid,' Frida said, 'I used to watch this TV show set in a country town. I can't remember the name of it, it was a kind of a soapie mystery series, but what I liked about it was that all the characters were completely different, but they all fitted in together. It was homely and safe. Sometimes I'd close my eyes and wish really hard that I could jump into the TV screen and live in their world.'

She was twisting her hands in her lap. 'I know it's kind of a weird goal, but that's what I want. To belong.'

'It's not weird at all,' I said. 'That's what I want, too.'

At 6 a.m. we went down to the lobby and I checked out while Frida waited by the front door. Her cap and sunglasses didn't quite hide her bruises.

"Let's get out of here,' she muttered as I joined her. 'The doorman is giving me some weird looks.'

CHAPTER ELEVEN

As I finished the last sentence of my email, Delroy appeared with my beer. I thanked him and he grinned back. 'You're welcome, Mr Forbes.' I was a regular at the Ocean Pearl—in the six months that Frida and I had been living in Port Antonio in Jamaica, it had become my favourite hotel. Perched on the side of a mountain, it looked through the lush jungle to a secluded bay.

We'd travelled here straight from Kingston, on the recommendation of a British expat we sat next to on the plane. Just to look around at first, but Frida and I both fell in love with it—the tropical languidness, fertile lushness, the chaotic shabbiness of the streets and shops and houses, the spontaneous and infectious joy of the people. A more dramatic contrast to Melbourne's buttoned up greyness would be hard to imagine. Like every city, it had its share of seediness and crime, but it was easy to ignore when you woke up every day to sunshine so bright it hurt your eyes and sky as blue as a child's drawing.

I took a sip of the beer. The coldness trickled down my throat and cooled my insides. The heat had taken a lot of getting used to. I was on the veranda. There was no air-conditioning, but a light afternoon breeze sprang up, taking the edge off the heat and drying my sweat-soaked shirt.

I re-read the email on the laptop I'd purchased in the ramshackle electronics shop in the main street. I'd told no one where I was and used a Virtual Private Network to hide my I. P. address.

'Mr Ron Viertel, Chairman of the Board, Palmer Products and Packaging. Dear Mr Viertel, I hereby tender my resignation as managing director of

Palmer Products and Packaging as of the date of this email.

Jackson Forbes.'

I had no qualms about this, but still my finger hovered over the mouse before I clicked 'send.' I knew after the first month I wasn't going back to Australia, but I requested extended leave from the Board, to allow the decision to percolate in my mind. But I didn't need an 'out' any longer and now was the time to pull the pin.

There was nothing for me to go back to. The cost of living was cheap here and Frida and I were still living off the cash we'd brought over. Two weeks after we arrived I received a furious email from Lindsay. Two heavies had accosted her in a hotel carpark after she'd had a night out with friends. They got into her car with her and demanded she tell them where I was.

'I was too angry to be frightened and I abused the hell out of them, told them I hated you and had no idea where you were and didn't care. Which wasn't far from the truth. I think I convinced them, but they took my phone anyway, the pigs. And one of them had the nerve to say, "I'm glad you're not my wife."'

Though I felt guilty about her being accosted, I couldn't help smiling. An angry Lindsay was a force to be reckoned with. And I was glad that for whatever reason the thugs had spared her the treatment they gave Carol. I wanted to tell her about Frida; she deserved to know the whole story, but I couldn't risk it. I replied to her email to apologise for the thugs and she accepted my apology with more grace than I deserved.

'I've come to the conclusion that you have a lot of demons from your past still inside you, and I hope that wherever you are and whatever you're doing, you can sort them out. For your sake, as well as that of any future women in your life.'

Since then, she'd taken my advice and sold the house, buying an apartment in St Kilda. Much more suited to her lifestyle. No mention of Hugh, so perhaps Kate's plan to force him to end the affair and manoeuvre him back into the family had come to fruition.

The big quandary hanging over me was that I'd killed one of Teff McGill's henchmen. Now he had double the reason to come after us. I did as much as

I could to cover our tracks, but these days it's almost impossible to disappear completely. And there's always someone prepared to divulge information for the right price. Most mornings I woke up drenched in sweat, and it wasn't solely the heat. But I pushed it to the back of my mind and got on with the day. I refused to let fear rule my life. We'd been here two months when I realised that my itching had stopped.

Through the palm trees fringing the turquoise waters of the bay, Frida and her boyfriend Jamero emerged. They'd been for a swim; Frida was wearing a cover-up over her bikini and Jamero was in board shorts, his broad black shoulders and chest gleaming in the sun. They stopped for a moment. He tilted her chin and kissed her on the lips.

As they approached the road, a group of cyclists came whizzing past. Jamero pulled Frida back quickly, his arm around her waist. Still with his arm around her, they crossed the road, then strolled up the path through the 100-foot banyan trees swaddled in vines towards the hotel.

Frida was a different person now. She'd filled out, the sharp planes of her face were softer and she sported a light golden tan. She'd lost that look of haunted wariness and when she smiled she revealed dimples I never knew she had. Her hair had grown to shoulder length and she'd had it styled properly, though she continued to dye it blonde, saying she preferred it that way. She certainly stood out with her blondness and dark eyes and eyebrows, and I knew it wouldn't take her long to find a man. I wasn't so sure about Jamero, though. He ran with a tough-talking, hard-partying crowd. But they'd only known each other for a couple of months, so time would tell.

They walked up the steps of the hotel, hand-in-hand.

'Good afternoon, sir,' Jamero said.

I'd told him countless times that the Queen hadn't knighted me, but he persisted in calling me sir. Perhaps he thought it was a way of winning my respect, but it would take a lot more than deference to do that. Especially where Frida was concerned.

'Would you like a drink?' I said.

'Haven't got time,' Frida said. 'I start work in an hour.'

She'd scored a job as a waiter at The Happy Parrot, a popular tourist restaurant in the main street. She was so efficient the owner was more than happy to pay her cash in hand, no questions asked. I expected she'd be running the place before too long. When he wasn't playing in his techno-reggae-rap band, Jamero worked as a barman at the Casino up the road—not that I ever went there or had any desire to visit the place.

'Do you need a lift home?' I asked.

'I can give her a lift, sir,' Jamero said. He caught my eye. 'I mean, Jackson, sir.'

Frida smiled at my expression, leaned over and gave me a hug. 'See you later, Dad.'

'I'll pick you up at the normal time—11 o'clock.'

'Goodbye sir,' Jamero said.

I ordered another beer and a dish of jerk chicken. This traditional Jamaican favourite didn't come any better than at this hotel, where they cooked it out the back over wood from the pimento tree on a traditional Jamaican grill. As I relished every piquant mouthful, I watched the shadows deepen over the bay, inhaled the sweet jungle air and listened to the screeching evening chorus of the parrots.

I paid the bill and waved goodbye to Delroy. 'See you tomorrow!' he called out. I got on my motorbike and negotiated the narrow winding road home. It was just a small 500 ml, all I needed here. The roads were rough, full of potholes and as unpredictable as the drivers. Much as I loved exploring the hidden bays and jungled valleys and hills, I missed the power of my BMW and roaring along on the open road. It had been impounded at Tullamarine Airport; Lindsay paid for its release and sold it at a fraction of what it was worth. All I hoped was that its new owner was getting as much pleasure from it as I had.

It was dark by the time I arrived at our colourful tumbledown wooden house, in a street full of houses exactly the same. The owner, a British expat who lived in Kingston (a friend of the man on the plane, who'd given me his details), let us have it for a nominal rent in exchange for renovating it and getting control of the runaway garden.

I spent my days haggling over prices with the locals at the lumberyard and the paint shop, re-building the porch, erecting a garden shed and clearing, hacking and slashing in the back yard. My experience working with Monty in his home renovation business all those years ago was being put to good use. I enjoyed doing physical work again, and when my back or knees hurt at the end of the day it was an honest, satisfying pain. Frida had planted a vegetable garden and already we could see the fruits of her labours—a row of cabbages uncurling to the sun like sea anemones, vines laden with tomatoes, fat, shiny sweet peppers and huddles of bok choi.

I parked my bike in the back yard, went inside and flicked on the lights. The paintwork was faded and the wooden floorboards were rickety, but with its bright yellow and green cupboards, timber panelling and linoleum floors in the kitchen and bathroom, the house had a certain retro appeal, which I'd enhanced with second-hand furniture.

As I passed Frida's bedroom to go to the bathroom, I glanced in through the open door. On the bedside table a brown apple core perched on top of a mess of jewellery and make-up, her towel and swimmers were draped over her open wardrobe door, and her clothes were on the floor where she'd just stepped out of them. A pile of papers lay on her rumpled bed. I went in and picked them up.

They were sketches in charcoal pencil, all in black and white. A branch of a breadfruit tree in the back yard, sprouting its golf ball-textured fruit, an empty seat overlooking the beach, a plump parrot perched in a tangle of vine, the silhouette of a woman looking up at the moon.

The lines were strong and fluid, the shading executed perfectly. Her style had become bolder and more confident—not that I'd seen much of her art. She would never let me see it. 'I'll show you when I'm happy with it,' she always said.

The last sketch in the pile was of a man slumped in an armchair, asleep, with his head back and mouth open. His hair was a tousled mess and his cheeks were gaunt. I took a few seconds to realise it was me. Crashed out in the tatty wingback armchair in front of our small TV, nestled in its dented pine cabinet. My default position. I was still getting used to hard labour; by 8 o'clock I'd had it. Did I really look that old?

I'd lost weight and had to admit I was looking a tad scrawny, though tanned from all my outdoor work, and I'd let my hair grow. Perhaps I looked old to Frida, the way all fathers seem old to their children. I studied the drawing again and my heart swelled. I placed the pile of drawings on her bed exactly as I'd found them.

My phone beeped. A text message from Carol. I'd disposed of my mobile phone before the flight to Jamaica, and now I used burner phones, discarding them and buying a new one every month. I went out on to the back porch overlooking my mostly-tamed garden and lowered myself into the sagging canvas chair under the light to read it.

'Hi Jack. I haven't heard from you since my last text. I hope you're not mad at me. Please reply.'

I clicked on the message she'd sent a week ago and read it again for the umpteenth time. 'Hi Jack, glad to hear that you and Frida are both safe. Are you coming back to Oz any time soon? I miss my little girl. There's something I have to tell you. I lied to you—while we were on the farm I screwed Tom. Those couple of times you went into town. It just happened, I was feeling so good and I wanted to thank him for letting us stay. I'm really sorry. For what it's worth, I know that Frida is your daughter.'

It didn't surprise me; I think in my subconscious I was half-expecting it. Carol always used sex to get what she wanted from men. Love, approval, admiration. She couldn't relate to them in any other way. I pictured Tom— tall, a farmer's rough-hewn build, dark hair, brown eyes.

I'd mulled over it all that week, watching Frida when she wasn't looking. Were those eyebrows Tom's? Her nose? Was that his impatience, the way she tapped her feet when waiting? In the end, it didn't matter. Biology didn't come into it. I sent a text message back to Carol.

'I'm not mad at you. As far as I'm concerned Frida is my daughter. I haven't told her what you said and I don't intend to.'

#

At 10.30 p.m. I set out on foot for The Happy Parrot. It was a few blocks from home and sometimes I picked Frida up on the motor bike, but the traffic was always bedlam in town on Saturday nights. There was often some sort of festival going on with the streets blocked off and it was easier to walk. I always made a point of picking her up; I didn't like her walking home by herself.

In the town centre, I pushed my way through the throngs of people singing and dancing in the street. Young men in baggy pants and loud shirts, generously proportioned women scantily clad in sequins and feathers, jiggling their breasts and wiggling their arses, children weaving in and out of the crowd, munching on pastries or slurping on bags of juice. A traditional calypso band was competing for attention with a brass band, playing a kind of reggae jazz. I had no idea what the festival was celebrating; not that it mattered. It was about joy and music and laughter; have fun today, tomorrow will take care of itself. Crowds bustled in front of tents spewing out fragrant aromas of barbecued meat, spices and coconut.

Next to one of the tents, Jamero's band was set up on a makeshift stage. He was on the drums, and I watched his powerful forearms and his nimble fingers as they flew to the rhythm. He had his eyes closed and he was nodding his head in time to the beat. As if he sensed me watching him, he opened his eyes, his face split into a grin and he waved. I waved back and kept going.

The night was muggy and I was sweating by the time I reached The Happy Parrot, a wooden shack painted in tropical colours with a huge parrot weathervane adorning the roof. I peered in through the gingham-curtained window. It was packed; a couple of waiters sauntered around. No one hurries in this country.

I spied Frida talking to a grey-haired man at a large table of well-fed, middle-aged couples, typical tour bus types. Their flushed, jovial faces were testament to the number of wine bottles on the table. As Frida walked away, the grey-haired man's gaze followed her rear until she stopped at the bar. He nudged the man sitting beside him, they both looked over at her, and the other man gave a leer.

I swallowed the anger that burned in my chest. It was irrational; they were just ignorant tourists, but it was borne of my instinct to protect Frida. Though she'd laugh at me if I told her so, telling me she could look after herself.

I bought a rum punch from a nearby roadside stall and downed it in a couple of gulps. Refreshment with a kick. I wasn't too fond of rum before I arrived, but I soon re-educated my palate. I'm sure Jamaicans would have rum for breakfast if they could work out how to cook ackee and saltfish in it.

Frida appeared at 11.20. She was invariably late; there always seemed to be a last minute crisis. She looked tired, but not the drawn tiredness of ongoing stress; it was the satisfied tiredness at the end of a hard day's work.

'Busy night?' I said.

She nodded. 'Yeah, a table full of mouthy Yank tourists, but I put them in their place.'

I grinned. 'I bet you did.'

We wove our way through the crowd. Noisy, messy, colourful. It summed up life in Jamaica perfectly. As we passed Jamero's band, he waved to her and beckoned her to come up on the stage with him. She shook her head, mimed going to sleep and blew a kiss to him.

'See you tomorrow,' she mouthed.

Jamero looked crestfallen. Besotted as she was with him, Frida still kept a certain part of herself in reserve. That was her nature, and in this case I was glad. I'd seen women give over their whole lives to a man and get hurt, and the last thing I wanted was for her to be so caught up in a relationship that she didn't have time for her dad.

We rounded the corner into the street a block from ours. The noise of the festival receded but people were still out and about in the streets. Ambling, laughing, dancing.

I put my arm around Frida's waist and gave her a squeeze. 'I'm glad you found me.'

She looked up at me, smiled and kissed me on the cheek. 'So am I.'

At that moment, all was right with the world. Ahead of us two Jamaican women sashayed up the street, swinging their ample hips, clapping and singing. A man came into view, striding towards us. His cap was pulled down over his face and he was wearing a jacket.

Who wears a jacket in this weather? I thought. As my mind screamed, 'Danger!' the man drew a gun out of his pocket and fired. Frida pitched forward without a sound and crumpled to the ground. A woman screamed.

A male voice behind me said, 'What the hell ? ...'

I crouched down and cradled her in my arms. 'Frida! Don't die!'

An engine rumbled. Brakes screeched. I got up and lunged at the man. 'You fucking bastard!' He leapt into the front passenger seat of a black sedan and it roared off. Its lights were off and it had no number plate, but under the street light I glimpsed the killer's face under his cap. Narrow, hooked nose, thin lips.

EPILOGUE

A car horn honks behind me and I jump. I've wandered on to the road without realising it. I move on to the footpath and wave a hand in apology as a beat-up VW full of grinning teenagers rattles past me.

It's been three and a half months and I'm still walking around in a cloud of grief. Anger is never far below the surface. Anger that McGill didn't shoot me as well. At first I couldn't work out why. Did he want to lull me into a false sense of security, then come back and finish me off? Then it came to me—death would give me release. Better to keep me alive and make me suffer. Even though he's not here to witness it, the satisfaction of retribution is still his.

I hit the bottle for a while and sometimes I'd stagger out into the road in the middle of the night and yell, 'Come and get me, you bastard! Kill me now!' until all the windows in the neighbourhood lit up and old Lateica from next door shuffled out, put her arm around my shoulder and escorted me inside.

My rational self told me there was no way I could have prevented the shooting, but I ignored it. I'd let her down, my daughter. I'd killed Arthur O'Keefe, let Sam die and now Frida was dead because I'd failed to protect her. Her last moments were in my mind when I passed out on the living room couch and first thing when I woke up.

Carol was just as much of a basket case when I phoned her with the news. In our first few conversations, all she did was sob uncontrollably down the phone. Last week she told me she'd given up drugs. 'I haven't had anything for six weeks. I have to stay clean for Frida. That's what she would have wanted.'

'What's the point now?' I yelled. 'She won't care, she's fucking dead. Why didn't you do it when she was alive?' Then I punched the 'end call' button. I phoned her back later to apologise.

'It's okay,' Carol said. 'You had a point, I should have done it when she was alive. But I didn't and I'm doing it now.'

I arrive at Errol's fruit shop, a little stall on the side of the road crammed with trays of every exotic fruit imaginable, from mangoes and guavas to star apples and breadfruit. I don't need any more fruit, but this is my daily walk. I force myself to get out of the house every day.

Errol's part-Indian, gentle and softly spoken. 'You're looking much better, Mr Jack,' he says.

'Looks can be deceiving,' I reply. The smile vanishes from his face and I'm immediately contrite for my snarky attitude. 'Actually, I am feeling a lot better since I cut down the drinking.'

'You need more Vitamin C.' He piles some assorted fruit into a large paper bag and hands it to me. I go to get my wallet out of my pocket, but Errol puts his hand up. 'On the house.'

I know he can't afford to give away his produce, but he'd be hurt if I refused. It's just one of many kindnesses shown to me over the past few weeks by people in my neighbourhood.

'Have you heard from the police?' Errol asks.

I shake my head. I don't expect to, not that I'll tell him that. The police arrived within minutes of the shooting, questioned the witnesses, took me to the police station and gave me a thorough grilling. Why would a man she didn't know shoot my daughter? I pretended to be as puzzled as they were; told them I thought it was a case of mistaken identity.

If they were suspicious that I knew more than I was letting on, they didn't express it and I think they've now put it in the too hard basket. The police here have a tradition of inefficiency and antiquated procedures. Which suits me. Teff would have been on the first plane out of the country after he shot Frida. If anyone is going to avenge her death, it will be me.

When I arrive home, Jamero is sitting on my newly built and painted front steps. I'd phoned him earlier and asked him to call around. 'Hey, Mr Jack!'

He's so traumatised he's stopped calling me 'sir.' For the first few weeks after Frida's death, he would wrap his massive arms around me whenever we met and sob like a child on my shoulder. Now he smiles but it doesn't reach the sadness in his eyes.

'I've got something for you,' I say, as I unlock the front door. He follows me inside and I dump the paper bag on the kitchen bench. I go into Frida's bedroom and return with a single sheet of sketch pad paper. I hand it to Jamero. 'I found this while I was cleaning out her room.'

It's a sketch of Jamero playing the drums. Frida had flawlessly captured the muscled tension of his body, the power in his raised arms, the fanatical gleam in his eye when he was in the heart of the music, riding the beat.

'I'm sure she meant to give it to you. She always wanted her drawings to be perfect before she let anyone see them.'

Jamero looks up, his eyes shining with tears. 'It is perfect.' He gives me another of his bear hugs. 'Thank you, Mr Jack. I'm so happy to have something to remember her by.'

As he turns to go, I say, 'Perhaps we could drop the 'mister' now.'

He grins. 'Sure, Mr Jack. See you later.'

He bounds down the front steps. The house feels lifeless again, despite the makeover I've given it. I've been working like a man possessed on the renovations and have finally finished them. New paint inside and out, remodelled kitchen and bathroom, and a workshop in the back yard where I can do some woodwork.

It looks so fresh and new that all the neighbours are asking me if I can do their houses, so I may have a flourishing business here. Most of them don't have much money, so it will be a case of bartering—a new porch in exchange for a freezer full of chickens. That's fine by me.

For a while I wondered if I should escape to another country, now that Teff knows where I am. There's no guarantee he won't come back and complete his revenge. But it's no life always looking over your shoulder, seeing a killer in every man or woman.

And what Teff McGill doesn't know is I'll have the last laugh. I'm living with my grief, but if I'm destined to die tomorrow, I don't care. Which could, given the right circumstances, make me dangerous and Teff a marked man.

I return to Frida's room and sit on the wooden chair near her window. I often come in here to be close to her. The room is tidy now, with the bed neatly made as if waiting for her to come and visit. Her drawings are gone— I bundled them all up and posted them to Carol. She'll be happy to know her daughter inherited her talent after all.

Except for the sketch of me asleep in the armchair. I've had it framed and it hangs in pride of place on the living room wall. It makes me smile every time I walk past it.

Get my e-book of four short crime stories *On The Edge* by

becoming a subscriber to Storey-Lines.

Go to http://storey-lines.com for your free copy now

I would really appreciate it if you could take a few minutes to put an honest review of Secret Kill on the site you bought it from. Reviews help other readers to decide whether they will enjoy the book, as well as helping it to gain more visibility and consequently, more sales.

ACKNOWLEDGMENTS

I have a number of people in my support crew to thank – my partner Aaron, for his love and help with all things technical and brainstorming plot ideas with me, my family for their moral support and my longstanding critique partner Pam Mariko for her constant and invaluable feedback.

I am also grateful to fellow author and beta reader Leeza Baric for her support and helpful comments (and for the title of this novel) and editor Richard Butler.

OTHER BOOKS BY ROBIN STOREY

For other books in the Noir Nights series and Robin's stand-alone novels, please visit Storey-Lines http://storey-lines.com or find Robin Storey on Amazon or IngramSpark.

E-books are available at all major e-book retailers.

ABOUT THE AUTHOR

Robin Storey is an indie author who lives on the picturesque Sunshine Coast in Queensland, Australia. She's a former freelance writer who is hooked on writing novels – it's the most challenging, but also the most satisfying thing she's done.

Robin is a certified book nerd and recharges her creative batteries by getting out into nature – hiking and chilling out at the beach.

Robin's favourite social media site is Facebook, so please go over and like her page and connect with her there.
https://www.facebook.com/RobinStoreywriter

She is also present on:

Twitter
https://twitter.com/RobinStorey1

Pinterest
http://pinterest.com/robinstorey

LinkedIn
http://www.linkedin.com/in/robinstoreyauthor

Instagram
https://instagram.com/robinstorey55/

YouTube
https://www.youtube.com/user/RobinStoreyAuthor

Goodreads
http://www.goodreads.com/author/show/7057008.Robin_Storey

www.ingramcontent.com/pod-product-compliance
Lightning Source LLC
Chambersburg PA
CBHW030654110726
47901CB00002B/706